CW00550358

For everyone who knew the answer
but didn't put their hand up.

THROUGH A LOOKING GLASS DARKLY

A REIMAGINING OF LEWIS CARROLL'S ORIGINAL TEXT
BY JAKE FIOR

ILLUSTRATED BY JOHN TENNIEL

ALICE LOOKING LONDON

Chapter One

One thing was certain, Mum was not going to be impressed. Alice had already suspected that the maths test mightn't have gone too well, but 48% was properly bad and the worst mark she'd been given for any subject in years.

'Well, I suppose I don't have to mention it unless Mum asks,' thought Alice. But Mum was sure to ask. Mum always asked. Everything was more difficult now that Dad wasn't there to help and at the moment she missed him terribly. But nobody was allowed to see that, not even Mum.

Alice had decided she was going to get a place at university and ride on a bicycle to her lectures. She wanted an old-style model with a basket at the front to put her books in and a loud bell to scare the tourists if they dawdled on the zebra crossing. Alice had definite plans for the future but this was now and for now she would have to walk.

Alice always chose the same route home from school in summer, cutting through the park to join the High Street from the gates at the north end. This was considered the less desirable stretch where a lot of the old businesses had closed down and a clutch of charity shops had opened up in their place.

Alice would browse in these for old books and treasure on the days that she had enough time and money to spend. She loved mysteries, to read the names previous owners had written in books and to imagine the journeys these volumes might have had before she came to meet with them. The first shop she went in was in aid of a heart disease charity and most of the space was given over to old clothes. As a result, there was a rather musty smell when you opened the door. Alice just quickly scanned the rails in this one in case she saw something special or vintage. She wasn't as bothered about fashion as most of the other girls at school but some of the designer labels could be re-sold on the internet for a profit and that would help her contribute towards the bills at home.

It seemed nothing interesting had come in since her last visit, so she thanked the assistant for letting her look around and continued on her way. The next shop was more mixed and for one pound Alice bought an old book about an explorer who travelled all the way to Africa to look for a river. It had a striking cover showing a large sailing boat moored off some exotic coast. 'Maybe it's Zanzibar?' thought Alice. She didn't know much about Zanzibar except that it was in Africa and had her favourite sounding name of any country. The shop Alice visited last was the Peacehaven Hospice shop.

This was the shop Alice liked best. The window was cluttered with an array of objects, arranged seemingly without thought to their neighbours. A brightly coloured abstract painting that looked as if it might be titled Portrait of a Headache had been placed next to a crumpled top hat, there were piles of LP records, CDs, a few board games, a stack of floral tiles, a set of rusting dumbbells and today amongst these misprized possessions, hidden away at the back and glinting mysteriously, stood a beautiful, dusty old mirror.

Graham, the shop manager, knew Alice by name and always greeted her arrival in the same theatrical manner.

'Welcome, curious Alice, come to look for curios?'

'Yes I am. I mean, I hope I'm welcome and yes, I am looking for something. The mirror in the window, can you tell me how much it is please?'

'Ah, madam has impeccable taste but is mistaken, for that is no mere mirror, that is an antique looking glass.'

'But what's the difference, apart from the name obviously?' asked Alice.

'Well, a mirror is just a shiny thing that reflects the sheer ghastliness of the modern world. A looking glass on the other hand is for looking in. For looking at yourself within. And as to price, it's thirty English pounds, which is cheap to those who can afford it and expensive to those who can't. I've only just put it in there. It came from a very grand house.'

Alice had nearly forty pounds saved up in her bike fund so she could just about afford it, however as it didn't seem cheap to her maybe she couldn't afford it after all? But she did want it.

Alice had always wanted a full length mirror so she could see her shoes and her top at the same time and not only that, this one was beautiful. It had an ornate gold frame with a pattern made of crosses and triangles carved into it. University was a long way off and although she didn't really think she meant to, Alice heard herself say out loud, 'Graham I want to buy it but it's a bit too big to carry. Is there any possible way you could deliver it home for me?'

Graham looked at Alice a while before conceding, 'I think

that could be arranged. I've brought the car in with me today and we close in ten minutes so let's say you pay me, write your new address on this receipt, and I'll meet you there in twenty minutes.'

As Alice hurried home her thoughts raced with her. 'How did I just blurt that out? "Graham I want to buy it, but it's a bit too big…" and it's a bit too 75% of all the money I have in the world!' Her maths was good enough to know that sum.

Graham had been around to Alice's old house to collect some of Dad's things but the new flat was much smaller and she hoped that he wouldn't comment on it. Alice wasn't ashamed of her surroundings though.

Dad had always taught her that she was as good as anyone and that if she worked hard and followed her dreams there was nobody and nothing that could stop her.

Graham helped Alice stand the looking glass up against the wall in the living room before he left. Now her heart beat a little faster as she tore the brown wrapping paper carefully away. The golden frame beneath the paper was even more impressive than she had remembered it. As well as the unusual pattern, there were columns on either side and carved at its base were the initials DEDI.

'How strange,' thought Alice. 'I wonder what that stands for?' As she leaned the looking glass away from the wall to free the last piece of wrapping from underneath, she noticed a small label stuck to the back of the frame. It had the number 63 printed in one corner and an inscription that read: 'Purchased for Stella Matutina from the Dodgson sale of 1898. Thought to have once been the property of Bishop Berkeley.'

'Purchased for Stella Matutina,' Alice repeated the words to

4

herself aloud. 'Stel-la Ma-tu-ti-na. What a lovely name. It sounds almost musical.'

Alice thought about her own name, Liddell. It seemed a bit dull by comparison. 'Maybe when I go to university I'll tell people it's pronounced Lidd-elle and that I own a looking glass that once belonged to a Bishop.'

The Bishop jogged Alice's memory. Lionel had sent her a new move in their chess game, Bishop captures Rook on g1, and she had still to make her own move in response. They had met at her previous school's chess club and kept in touch by playing correspondence chess online. Alice had gone to the club on the days Mum was going to be late home from work and was one of the few girls that played there. Some of the other girls thought Alice a bit of a geek for going but she wasn't bothered. They all just dressed the same way and did the same boring things together. Alice liked Lionel, but he had recently started inviting her out on dates and she didn't like him in that kind of a way. She was running out of excuses and it was tricky but Alice decided as she hadn't done anything to encourage him, at the end of this game she was just going to have to tell him how it was. It seemed unfair, thought Alice, that somehow good-looking boys were never very interesting and interesting boys were never very good-looking.

Alice turned her attention back to her chess game. 'Bishop captures Rook. Hmm, I wonder why he's done that?'

She decided to leave her reply for later as she was feeling quite tired and didn't want to rush and make a mistake.

As she turned away from the computer she noticed something else about her new looking glass. The mirror surface had begun to shimmer a strange shade of blue.

'That's odd,' thought Alice. 'There's only white light bulbs in here so maybe that colour is coming from outside?' But outside was getting darker and now the looking glass was getting brighter. Alice took a few steps forward and looked at herself fully within its frame for the very first time. Her reflection stared back at her quizzically. Something weird was definitely happening, but what exactly was it? As Alice edged closer, it seemed the room in the mirror was beginning to cloud with mist while the air around her remained completely clear. 'That's probably just condensation on the glass from my breath,' she told herself.

Alice gingerly stretched out her right arm to touch the frosted surface but to her astonishment felt her hand pass right through the wall and into the empty space beyond. The air was colder on the other side and Alice could feel the hairs on her arm begin to stand up. 'Could this really be happening?' she asked herself, it didn't seem possible. Alice took a deep breath and tried to work out what to do next. 'If I try to go through the glass and this isn't real, then I'll find out with a bump pretty quickly,' she reasoned.

Alice carefully lifted her right foot up and through the frame without resistance and before long her whole body was on the other side of the wall. The mist was lifting now and Alice's eyes gradually adjusted to her new surroundings. To her surprise, Alice found she was standing on the mantelpiece of a large marble fireplace. The rest of the room was almost the same but looked different, older. Using her left arm to support her weight Alice jumped carefully down to the floor and looked around. The furniture here was heavy and brown instead of the light colours she was used to at home and it seemed to be winter on this side of the glass. Even the sunflowers in Mum's print looked as if they were swaying under a real breeze.

A clock on the mantelpiece counted out time with a reassuring tick, whilst in a silver ashtray, wisps of smoke curled gently from the tip of a still smouldering cigarette. Whoever had been here had not been gone long. Over by the window there was a mahogany writing desk with some notepaper stacked neatly upon it and weighted down by a carefully placed ink pen.

Curious as to what might have been written, Alice walked up and examined the work of the anonymous author.

However, all that was there was the one lonely question, 'will she ever return?' carefully lettered in purple ink on the top sheet. Alice was not sure that she wanted to stay in this new world but was too fascinated to leave straight away. She glanced back toward the looking glass. It was then that she caught sight of her own reflection and realised things were getting even stranger. While she herself still looked the same, her clothes had somehow become old fashioned. In fact they were so unfashionable they could have been out of style one hundred years ago.

Suddenly in the reflection of the glass, Alice glimpsed a sinister looking shadow dart across the opposite wall. She reeled round, scanning the room in an effort to try and locate whatever had cast it but could see nothing. Although the room was still, Alice had the uncomfortable feeling that she was being watched. Down in front of the fire lay what looked like an unfinished chess game with some of the pieces carelessly discarded around the board.

Alice bent down to take a closer look but was totally unprepared for the scene of carnage that was to greet her. Mangled bodies were strewn amongst the squares, pawns lay outstretched on their sides, serene as if in sleep but without breathing and the Knight, the Knight was on his back, only just alive, his body broken and his face wracked with pain. Alice wanted to turn her head away but his gaze met hers and beckoned her closer.

He summoned his last strength and with it whispered gravely 'Beware....you must beware the Jabberwock.'

'The Jabberwock?' Was it this Jabberwock that had done these terrible things?

'What is a Jabberwock?' she asked the Knight but he lay silent.

'This is just mad!' thought Alice, but it was happening.

A loud cough interrupted her thoughts. Alice jumped up startled to see a small King dressed in red robes emerge trembling from under a pile of ashes in which he'd been hiding. Despite having to dust the dirt from his clothing, the King immediately assumed an imperious tone.

'Who and what are you? And why do you not curtsey? It is important to observe protocol even in the most unpleasant of circumstances.'

'My name is Alice Liddell and I'm from Hammersmith in London.'

The Red King looked up at Alice and shook his head as if he were inspecting a particularly unsatisfactory parade soldier.

'It is written that a male child will come from beyond the borderland to defeat the foul beast, but alas you cannot be the one for you are only a girl.'

Alice was angry. This coward who had clearly hidden during the onslaught was now being rude about her and they'd never even met before. 'He's wrong and old fashioned like everything else around here,' thought Alice. 'I'm not only a girl.'

'If you don't mind sir, I'm not just a girl, I'm a girl who's a good deal bigger than you are, so maybe I will fight this horrid beast for you after all?' Alice didn't know why she had said this and it was quite a bold statement from someone that had only ever had one real fight in her entire life.

Lyndsey Taylor started out being quite friendly when Alice first joined St Jerome's.

She had even invited Alice to join her small clique of friends, but although Alice tried to be polite, her refusals had not gone down well at all. It started off gradually with some remarks in the dinner queue but quickly turned to taunts about Alice's taste in music on her profile page and after that her locker got broken into and had insults and expletives daubed on the inside. Alice tried hard to ignore all of these events but it only seemed to encourage more of them, then Lyndsey had started saying those things about Dad in the corridor after physics and that was it. Alice didn't even remember doing half of the things she was accused of as it was all a bit of a blur, but both she and Lyndsey were suspended for a day. Apparently, Lyndsey's parents had threatened to sue the school claiming her nose was no longer perfectly straight and this could damage a future modelling career. Mum said they should be happy as it would give Lyndsey a more edgy look and anyway the swelling would go down in a couple of days, but she made Alice promise not to fight with anyone again.

'I sincerely wish that you could help,' said the King, 'but look upon the table. There lies the Book of Truths, open it and you may come to understand.'

Sure enough there was a small leather bound book on a side table near Alice. Keeping one eye suspiciously on the King, she quickly leafed through the pages. The title read YKCOWREB-BAJ which reminded her of something, although Alice was not sure why since she had never seen a language quite like it. She stared at the letters intently. COWREB was almost like cobweb but she didn't think YKCOWREBBAJ meant anything at all.

Alice tried re-arranging the letters and found the words BABY and CROW but that still left the E and the J.

Then it came to her. All the letters were back to front. Alice hurried excitedly with the book to the looking glass and held it up. The word revealed was JABBERWOCKY and underneath was a poem:

'Twas brillig, and the slithy toves
Did gyre and gimble in the wabe;
All mimsy were the borogoves,
And the mome raths outgrabe.

'Beware the Jabberwock, my son !
The jaws that bite, the claws that catch !
Beware the Jubjub bird, and shun
The frumious Bandersnatch!'

He took his vorpal sword in hand:
Long time the manxome foe he sought --
So rested he by the Tumtum tree,
And stood awhile in thought.

And as in uffish thought he stood,
The Jabberwock, with eyes of flame,
Came whiffling through the tulgey wood,
And burbled as it came!

One two! One, two! And through and through
The Vorpal blade went snicker-snack!
He left it dead and with its head
He went galumphing back.

"And hast thou slain the Jabberwock ?
Come to my arms my beamish boy !
O frabjous day ! Callooh ! Callay ! "
He chortled in his joy

'Twas brillig and the slithy toves
Did gyre and gimble in the wabe,
All mimsy were the borogroves,
And the mome raths outgrabe.'

The King clearly thought these bizarre verses held some sort of prophecy. He was hoping for a beamish boy, whatever that might be, and Alice had disappointed him.

Sometimes Alice thought Dad had wanted a boy. He had told her that was nonsense but it hadn't stopped him from sometimes treating her a bit like one.

He took her sword fencing with him and taught her both foil and sabre but, although she became quite proficient with both, Alice had preferred the Saturday afternoons when they would sit and paint together in his studio.

'I'm afraid I didn't understand all of the poem,' announced Alice apologetically.

'Sadly there are always more puzzles than answers,' said the King gesturing towards a sash window through which Alice could see a large formal garden. Some of the beds were overgrown with wild flowers and the trees had begun to shed their leaves which gathered in vivid autumnal colours on the ground beneath.

'The dim shadows of those trees are the Jabberwock's domain,' he added grimly.

'Then I suppose that is where I will have to go,' answered Alice as she pulled back her hair and tied it with a velvet ribbon she had found in the pocket of the pinafore she was wearing.

In the corner of the room was a wooden staircase and as Alice placed her foot onto the first step, it folded under itself and lurched into a loud rumbling motion, descending like a noisy escalator. At the bottom she found a door swung open on its hinges and beyond that was the garden.

Alice stepped out of the house and quickly surveyed her surroundings. As well as the flowerbeds she had seen from the window there was a small disused stone fountain in the shape of a swan and in the near distance a hill.

Chapter Two

Alice decided she would make for the hill. It was a good vantage point from which to get a view of the surrounding area and luckily there was a winding path which seemed to lead straight to it. But the further up the path she walked the more distant the hill became.

As she neared the top, the path suddenly wound sharply to the left and Alice found herself in front of the house again.

'There's no use wasting your time even talking about it,' she said, looking at the house and pretending it was arguing with her. 'I'm not going back yet, and that's final.'

So, turning away from the house Alice set out one more time up the path, determined to keep going until she got to the top. For a few minutes all went to plan and she was just thinking, 'All right, it looks like I'm actually going to manage it this time,' when the path gave an unexpected twist and the next moment she found herself walking back up to the same front door.

'Oh, this is just a complete pain!' Alice shouted. 'I've never known a house to keep getting in the way like this!'

However, there was the hill in full sight so there was nothing to do but start back out again. As she walked up toward the path she came upon a large flower-bed, bordered by daisies and tiger lilies with a solitary willow-tree growing in the middle. 'Tiger-lily,' said Alice, addressing one that was waving gracefully in the wind, 'I wish you could talk and give me some directions!'

'We can talk,' said the Tiger-lily, 'when there's anybody worth talking to.'

Alice was so amazed that she didn't know what to say in reply. After a while, as the Tiger-lily only went on waving about, she spoke again, almost in a whisper and asked, 'Can all the flowers talk?'

'As well as I can,' said the Tiger-lily. 'And a great deal louder than you.'

'It isn't good manners for us to begin, you know,' said the Rose, 'and I really was wondering when you'd speak! Said I to myself, "Her face has got some sense in it, though it's not a clever one!" Still, you're the right sort of colour, and that can go a long way around here.'

'I don't care about the colour,' the Tiger-lily remarked. 'If only her petals curled up a little more, she'd be all right.'

Although Alice was quite amazed by these talking flowers she didn't particularly like being criticised just because of her appearance, so started asking some questions of her own. 'Aren't you lot sometimes frightened by being planted outside, with nobody to take care of you?'

'There's the tree in the middle,' said the Rose. 'What else is it good for?'

'But what could that do if any dangerous characters came sneaking about?' asked Alice.

'It says bough-wough!' cried a Daisy. 'That's why its branches are called boughs!'

'Didn't you know that?' cried another Daisy, and here they all began shouting together till the air seemed full of shrill little voices.

'Silence, every one of you!' cried the Tiger-lily, waving itself violently from side to side, and shaking with anger. 'They know I can't get at them!' it panted, 'or they wouldn't dare to do it!'

'Never mind,' Alice said in a soothing tone, and stooping down to the daisies who were just beginning again she whispered, 'If you don't pipe down, I might just pick you for a daisy chain!'

There was instant silence and several of the white daisies turned pink.

'That's right!' said the Tiger-lily. 'The daisies are worst of all. When one speaks, they all begin together, and it's enough to make one wither to hear the way they go on!'

'How is it you can all talk so nicely?' Alice said, hoping to get it into a better mood with a compliment. 'I've been to lots of gardens before but none of the flowers could talk.'

'Put your hand down and feel the ground,' said the Tiger-lily. 'Then you'll know why.'

Alice did so. 'It's very hard,' she said, 'but I don't see what that's got to do with it.'

'In most gardens,' the Tiger-lily said, 'they make the beds too soft - so that the flowers are always asleep.'

Alice felt this sounded reasonable if not entirely convincing. 'I never thought of that before!' she said.

'It's my opinion that you never think at all,' the Rose said in a rather superior manner.

'I never saw anybody that looked stupider,' exclaimed a Violet suddenly.

16

'Hold your tongue!' cried the Tiger-lily. 'As if you ever saw anybody! You keep your head under the leaves and snore away there, till you know no more what's going on in the world than if you were a bud!'

'Are there any more people in the garden besides me?' asked Alice, as she was keen to steer the conversation towards a subject that might actually help her.

'There's one other flower in the garden that can move about like you,' said the Rose. 'I wonder how you do it - but she's more bushy than you are.'

'Is she like me?' Alice asked eagerly, for the thought crossed her mind that there was another normal girl in this garden somewhere.

'Well, she has the same awkward shape as you,' the Rose said, 'but she's redder -- and her petals are shorter, I think.'

'Her petals are done up close, almost like a dahlia,' the Tiger-lily interrupted: 'not tumbled about anyhow, like yours.'

'But that's not your fault,' the Rose added kindly: 'you're probably beginning to fade, you know -- and then one can't help one's petals getting a little untidy.'

Alice didn't want to talk about her hair so, to change the subject, she asked, 'Does she ever come out here, this girl?'

'I daresay you'll see her soon,' said the Rose. 'She's one of the thorny kind.'

'And where does she wear these thorns?' Alice asked with some curiosity.

'All round her head, of course,' the Rose replied. 'I was wondering why you hadn't got some too. I thought it was part of the regulations.'

'She's coming!' cried the Larkspur. 'I hear her footsteps,

crunch, scrunch, crunch, along the gravel!'

Alice looked round eagerly and found that it wasn't a girl but a Queen dressed in scarlet from head to foot. 'She's a lot taller than the Red King!' remarked Alice. Indeed the Red Queen was tall, maybe even taller than Alice herself.

'It's the fresh air that does it,' said the Rose: 'wonderfully fine air it is, out here.'

'I think I'll go and meet her,' said Alice, for, though the flowers were interesting company, she hadn't really got much sense out of them.

'You can't possibly do that,' said the Rose: 'I should advise you to walk the other way.'

This sounded like more nonsense to Alice so she said nothing and immediately set off towards the Red Queen. To her surprise, she lost sight of her in a moment, and found herself walking in at the front door again.

This was very frustrating but instead of shouting, Alice decided to stay calm and after looking everywhere for the Queen (whom she spied at last, a long way off), she thought she would try a new plan this time, of walking in the completely opposite direction.

This succeeded brilliantly. She had not been walking a minute before she found herself face to face with the Red Queen, and in full sight of the hill she had been trying to reach for so long.

'Where do you come from?' said the Red Queen. 'And where are you going? Look up, speak nicely, and don't twiddle your fingers all the time.'

Alice complied with all these directions, and explained, as well as she could, that she had lost her way.

'I don't know what you mean by your way,' said the Queen:

'all the ways about here belong to me -- but why did you come out here at all?' she added in a kinder tone. 'Curtsey while you're thinking what to say, it saves time.'

Alice was a little sceptical of this, but she was too confused by the Queen to completely disbelieve it. 'I'll try it when I go home,' she thought to herself, 'the next time I'm late for dinner.'

'It's time for you to answer now,' the Queen said, looking at her watch. 'Open your mouth a little wider when you speak and always say your beloved Majesty.'

'I only wanted to see what the garden was like, your Majesty—'

'That's right,' said the Queen, patting her on the head, which Alice didn't appreciate at all, 'though, when you say "garden," -- I've seen gardens, compared with which this would be a wilderness.'

Alice didn't argue the point but carried on, '-- and I thought I'd try and find my way to the top of that hill – '

'When you say "hill",' the Queen interrupted, 'I could show you hills, in comparison with which you'd call that a valley.'

'No, I wouldn't,' said Alice, surprised into contradicting her at last. 'That's nonsense, a hill can't ever be a valley, it has exactly the opposite meaning.'

The Red Queen shook her head, 'You may call it "nonsense" if you like,' she said, 'but I've heard nonsense, compared with which my last statement would be as sensible as a dictionary!'

Alice curtseyed again, as she was afraid from the Queen's tone that she was a little offended: and they walked on in silence through some trees till they got near the top of the hill.

For some minutes Alice stood without speaking, looking out in all directions over the country -- and a most weird country it was too.

There were a number of tiny little brooks running straight across it from side to side, and the ground between was divided up into squares by a number of little green hedges that reached from brook to brook.

'It's marked out just like a giant chessboard!' said Alice eventually. 'There are even some chessmen moving about over there! It's like a huge game of chess that's being played out -- all over the world -- if this is the world at all? If I could even get to be a Pawn then I could join in -- though of course it would be much better to be a Queen.'

She felt a little self-conscious about admitting this in front of a real Queen, but her companion only smiled pleasantly, and said,

'That's easily managed. You can be the White Queen's Pawn, if you like, she won't mind and you're in the Second Square to begin with: when you get to the Eighth Square you'll be a Queen – '

Just at this moment, somehow or other, they began to run.

Alice could not quite make out, when thinking it over afterwards, how it was that they began, all she remembered was that they were running hand in hand, and the Queen went so fast that it was all she could do to keep up with her, and still the Queen kept crying 'Faster! Faster!' but Alice could not go any faster. The most curious part of it was that the trees and the other things round them never changed their places at all. However fast they went, they never seemed to pass anything.

'I wonder if all the things move along with us?' puzzled Alice.

And the Queen seemed to guess her thoughts, for she cried, 'Faster! Don't try to talk!'

Not that Alice had any idea of doing that. She felt as if she would never be able to talk again, she was getting so out of breath and still the Queen cried, 'Faster! Faster!' and dragged her along.

'Are we nearly there yet?' Alice managed to pant out at last.

'Nearly there!' the Queen repeated. 'Why, we passed it ten minutes ago! Faster!' And they ran on for a time in silence, with the wind whistling in Alice's ears and almost blowing her hair off her head.

'Now! Now!' cried the Queen. 'Faster! Faster!' And they went so fast that they seemed to skim through the air, hardly touching the ground with their feet until suddenly, just as Alice was getting quite exhausted, they stopped, and she found herself sitting on the ground, breathless and giddy.

The Queen propped her up against a tree, and said kindly, 'You may rest a little now.'

Alice looked round her in great surprise. 'We've been under this tree the whole time! Everything's just the same as it was!'

'Of course it is,' said the Queen, 'how would you have it?'

'Well, in my country,' said Alice, still panting a little, 'you'd generally get to somewhere else -- if you ran very fast for a long time, as we've just been doing.'

'A slow sort of country!' said the Queen. 'Now, here, you see, it takes all the running you can do to keep in the same place. If you want to get somewhere else, you must run at least twice as fast as that!'

'I'd rather not try, please!' said Alice. 'I'm quite happy here though I am very hot and thirsty!'

'I know what you'd like!' the Queen said good-naturedly, taking a little box out of her pocket, 'a biscuit.'

Alice thought it would not be polite to say no though a biscuit wasn't what she wanted at all. So she took it, and ate it as best she could, though it was very dry and unappetising.

'While you're refreshing yourself,' said the Queen, 'I'll just take the measurements.' And she took a tape measure out of her pocket, marked in inches, and began measuring the ground, and sticking little pegs in here and there.

'At the end of two yards,' she said, putting in a peg to mark the distance, 'I shall give you your directions -- have another biscuit?'

'No, thank you,' said Alice: 'one's quite enough!'

'Thirst quenched, I hope?' said the Queen.

Alice did not know what to say to this, but luckily the Queen did not wait for an answer, but went on. 'At the end of three yards I shall repeat them -- for fear of your forgetting them. At the end of four, I shall say good-bye. And at the end of five, I shall go!'

She had got all the pegs put in by this time, and as Alice looked on with great interest the Queen returned to the tree, and then began slowly walking down the row. At the two-yard peg she faced round, and said, 'A pawn goes two squares in its first move, you know. So you'll go very quickly through the Third Square -- by railway, I should think -- and you'll find yourself in the Fourth Square in no time. Well, that square belongs to Tweedledum and Tweedledee -- the Fifth is mostly immaterial-- the Sixth belongs to Humpty Dumpty- the Seventh is a bun-fight - But you make no remark?'

'I didn't know I had to make one,' replied Alice, confused.

'You should have said, "It's extremely kind of you to tell me all this"-- however, we'll suppose it said -- the Eighth Square is in darkness -- however, one of the Knights will show you the way -- then we might be Queens together, where it's all feasting and fun!'

Alice got up and curtseyed, and sat down again. At the next peg the Queen turned again, and this time she said, 'Speak in French when you can't think of the English for a thing -- turn out your toes as you walk -- and remember who you are!' She did not wait for Alice to curtsey this time, but walked on quickly to the next peg, where she turned for a moment to say 'good-bye,' and then hurried on to the last.

How it happened, Alice never knew, but exactly as the Queen came to the last peg, she was gone. Whether she vanished into the air, or whether she ran quickly into the wood, there was no way of guessing, but she was gone, and Alice began to remember that she was a Pawn, and that it would soon be time for her to move.

Scrying, Catoptromancy, Crystallomancy, there had been many names given to the art down the ages. The ability to see the future in a glass, visions in a grain of sand.

From the Oracle of Petras to John Dee's experiments at the court of Queen Elizabeth, for centuries men had strived to discover secrets that had vanished with the flood. Now few of his kind remained, desolate and cast adrift in time.

April 25th 1900,
Montmartre

Paris almost felt like a different city on the left bank of its
river, the grand formal avenues gradually surrendered to
crowded lively boulevards where a hundred different accents
competed to be heard. Up above street level, different forces
stirred.

A narrow beam of sunlight crossed the small attic room and
lit up the dust that danced in its wake. Samuel Mathers stared
up into this strange manifestation for a sign as he considered
events of the past month. The London Temple was in open re-
volt, they had refused to acknowledge his last decree and were
now demanding to meet the Secret Chiefs in person. Like children squabbling over their turn in a trivial game when all the
while a great storm threatened, they had even attempted to vote
him out of his own Magical order, but any society without a hi-
erarchy invites chaos and the situation required decisive action.
He had dispatched a disciple to take control of the Temple and
bring him back the most treasured prize in all mysticism, The
Enochian Looking Glass. But now his plans lay in tatters and he
was being forced to question the motives of his own agent.
'Crowley!' It was an ugly sounding name thought Mathers,

like the caw of a bird that could not sing. The reputation preceding it was ugly too.

'A man of unspeakable life' was how DEDI chose to describe him, Mathers had remained unmoved. It was the job of poets to speak of life in every aspect. Petty morality was for prudes and hypocrites, not poets and magicians. But whatever the truth of Crowley's reputation, his actions had compromised the mission and the Looking Glass was gone. Why would he have chosen to arrive at the Hammersmith Temple dressed as Osiris? Did he think he would pass through the streets unnoticed, or was he so deluded that he felt able to cast himself invisible? Transformative spells were at the highest level of Sacred Magic and well beyond the powers of a relative novice like him.

Or had he intended to be discovered all along and in the midst of the commotion take the Looking Glass for his own sinister ends?

If Crowley had stolen it, he was in grave danger, because if you were not chosen to possess the Glass, over time it would possess you. For the Looking Glass was no mere crystal, it was the instrument to balance an entire universe.

Chapter Three

Now Alice was near the top she assumed running up the the hill again would bring her down its other side, but within a few steps she was at the very peak.

'That's funny,' thought Alice, 'or actually it isn't. When you get to the top you just come down the normal way.' And with that she ran down the hill and jumped over the first of the little brooks.

To her great surprise Alice landed not onto grass as she had expected, but straight into the passenger compartment of a moving locomotive.

'Tickets, please!' said the Guard, putting his head in at the window. And in a moment everyone in the carriage except Alice was holding out a large train ticket.

'Now then! Show your ticket, child!' the Guard angrily went on. And a great many voices said all together, 'Don't keep him waiting, child! Why his time is worth a thousand pounds a minute!'

'I'm afraid I haven't got one,' Alice apologised. 'There wasn't a ticket-office where I came from.'
Again the chorus of voices chimed in. 'There wasn't room for

one where she came from. The land there is worth a thousand pounds an inch.'

'Don't make excuses,' said the Guard. 'You should have bought one from the driver.'

And once more the chorus of voices added, 'The man that drives the train, why his sweat alone is worth a thousand pounds a drop.'

'It's pointless speaking to this Guard with his chorus of disapproval,' thought Alice.

The voices didn't pipe up this time as she hadn't spoken, but to her surprise they all thought in chorus too, 'Best to say nothing at all. Language is worth a thousand pounds a word!'

'I could dream about a thousand pounds tonight except it would probably cost two thousand pounds to dream it here,' was Alice's guess.

All this time the Guard was studying her closely, first through a telescope, then through a microscope and then through some binoculars. At last he said, 'You're travelling in the wrong direction!' slammed down the window and went away.

'A young girl,' said the gentleman sitting opposite (who was dressed in a white paper suit and hat) 'ought to know which way she's going, even if she doesn't know how to get there!' This statement seemed quite judgemental to Alice, coming as it did from someone with such an unusual fashion sense.

Sitting next to him was a Goat that closed its eyes and slowly intoned, 'She should know her way to a ticket-office even if she doesn't know about etiquette.'

Just then a hoarse sounding voice spoke up loudly from somewhere behind the Goat and shouted 'All Change!'

'That sounds like a horse,' thought Alice and an extremely

small voice close to her ear said, 'You could make a joke about that - like something about a hoarse horse.'

Then a very gentle voice in the distance said, 'she must be labelled Handle with Care, you know,' and after that different voices started adding their opinions saying, 'She must go by post as she's got a head on her.' 'She must be sent as a message, it's faster.' 'No, she should be made to drive the train herself for the rest of the way.'

Then the gentleman dressed in white leaned forward and whispered in her ear, 'Never mind what they all say, my dear, but get a return ticket every time the train stops.'

'Thanks for the advice but I most definitely will not,' said Alice impatiently. 'I don't belong on this train journey at all. I was in a wood just now, and I would very much like to get back there if you don't mind!'

'You could make a joke about that too.' said the little voice, 'something like "you would if you could."'

Alice looked about to see where the voice was coming from but couldn't work it out. 'Well, seeing as you're such a great comedian, why don't you make a joke yourself?' she said, addressing the invisible conversationalist.

'I know you are a friend, a kind friend with a good heart and you won't hurt me though I am an insect.'

'Oh, I wondered why I couldn't see you. Are you a flea? Don't tell me I should flee or suggest another one of your terrible jokes.'

'I am not a flea and it's no joke this time. They say you might be the special one but it's a bad place, the eighth square, try your best to remember it.'

Alice could hardly make this out as the already little voice was now talking in a whisper and it turned out that the hoarse sounding voice actually did belong to a horse because he stuck his long neck through from the back of the carriage and announced, 'There is no cause for alarm but can passengers please adopt the brace position as the train is shortly going to have to jump over a brook.'

'No cause for alarm?' thought Alice. 'He's just explained why we should all be very alarmed. But this will hopefully take me into the fourth square and anyway it doesn't seem as if there's really much choice.'

In the next moment she could feel butterflies stirring in her stomach as the train lifted steeply into the air. Alice grabbed out at the nearest thing to steady herself which unfortunately in this instance happened to be the Goat's beard. But the strands of his beard quickly melted into clouds and Alice found herself

31

floating suspended high above the ground.

'What a strange breed of goat,' thought Alice. 'I wonder what they call it?'

'My name, child, is Mithras and I would be grateful if in future you would kindly desist from pulling at my beard.'

She heard his voice not with her ears like she had before in the carriage, but somehow echoing around the inside of her head.

'As you can appreciate, you are now light enough to float above the sphere of your material concerns.'

Alice was starting to regret ever coming through the Looking Glass but before she had even finished thinking about it the Goat interrupted, 'In time you will find an answer to your fears for no destiny is ever written with a pen.'

'Maybe that's true,' thought Alice, 'but it's difficult to make sense of this place with its talking horses and jumping trains and now a goat that can speak in your mind with sentences that seem to mean both everything and nothing.'

'Today it appears confusing but eventually you will come to understand,' and with that the Goat lowered her gently to the ground and in the next moment was gone.

Alice was in two minds as to what to do next but although one side of herself was telling her to turn back, the other had already made the decision to go on.

She started out through open country and soon began to pass fields with crops rotting and un-harvested.

'What a waste,' thought Alice. 'Why would anyone work hard to farm the land and then just abandon it like that?'

Walking further brought her to a large empty field that was bordered at its perimeter by a line of jagged trees. The wood loomed dark and foreboding with a canopy of densely packed foliage that shut out the light like a great cloak. As Alice got closer she noticed a crudely fashioned sign in the shape of an arrow that pointed inwards. The sign had the words Nameless Wood painted on it in a rough, childish hand. Seeing this did nothing to quell Alice's growing sense of unease. 'It's a complete contradiction,' thought Alice. 'Why bother putting that there in the first place if the wood really has no name?' But what was really bothering Alice, was that she was beginning to feel nervous about going in. Alice reassured herself by whistling the tune of one of her favourite songs as she stepped cautiously under the trees... 'When you walked around the house wearing mascara and gloss…' She tried to think of more words but to her surprise she couldn't remember any,.. or the title, or even who it was by. Well, at least I'm in this,.. in this... what do you call it? And it doesn't seem quite so bad once you're in here.'

Alice stood thinking in silence for a moment before realising she didn't even know her own name, let alone some lyrics to a song. A little panicked she tried hard to remember but all she could think of was that it started with an L. She concentrated intently but still couldn't get any more letters. Whilst Alice was busily engaged in this, a Fawn wandered by. It looked at her with its large gentle eyes but didn't seem at all frightened.

'Hello, my darling,' said Alice softly and put out her hand to stroke it but the Fawn backed away a bit and only stood looking at her again.

'What do you call yourself?' the Fawn eventually asked Alice.

'I wish I knew,' Alice replied. 'I'm really nobody right now.'

'Think again,' said the Fawn, 'it won't do to call yourself that.'

Alice tried but nothing came to her. 'If you could tell me your name, I think it might help me remember mine.'

'I'll tell you if you come a little further with me. I can't tell you here,' was the Fawn's reply. So they walked on together through the wood, Alice with her arms clasped affectionately around the soft neck of the Fawn until they came out into another field and here the Fawn gave a sudden jump and shook itself free.

'I'm a Fawn,' it cried out joyfully and, 'Oh dear you're a human!' A sudden look of alarm came into its eyes and it bounded away.

'Come back you silly thing, I'm a vegetarian!' shouted Alice after it but too late. The Fawn was gone from sight.

'Well, I suppose I'm not really a proper vegetarian,' thought Alice, 'but I would never eat a deer, that's for sure, let alone a baby deer and my name's Alice – I remember that now too.'

There was a dirt road that ran alongside the field which had two signposts on it. One said To Tweedledum's house and the other said To the house of Tweedledee. With her memory re-turned, Alice was able to recall the Red Queen mentioning these names so it seemed at least she was on the right track, besides which there was only this one road and both signs point-ed along it in exactly the same direction.

'I'll decide which house to head towards when the road di-vides and the signs point in different directions,' thought Alice as she started out but although she walked for a long distance, when occasionally the road did fork, both signs still pointed ex-actly the same way.

'I think I've worked it out,' Alice told herself. 'They must live in the same house but both of them call it by a different name. I'll just drop by and introduce myself and get them to show me the way out of this wood. I think I'd definitely like to be out of here before it gets dark.'

Alice, remembering what the Red King had said about the shadows of the trees, started to quicken her pace.

Village of Foyers,
Scottish Highlands

Sheltered on a hill above the eastern shore of Loch Ness, the manor house was remote enough to draw little attention from prying eyes, but there were still whispers among the locals about its strange new owner.

Contrary to social convention, signs warning trespassers to 'keep off' were Mr Crowley's only concession to the fact that he had any neighbours at all, that and the savage dogs he let loose to patrol the estate.

He had arranged for the temple furniture to be transported from London by a professional removals company, but had insisted on packing and sealing all the crates alone. The workmen were paid and dismissed immediately upon arrival so as to minimise any time wasted in banalities. Even with these precautions, there was one object he refused to let out of his sight. Brought with him wrapped carefully in blankets and velvet, he had chosen to ride with it in the goods van of the train, despite being in possession of a First Class ticket.

On arrival at Edinburgh station he commanded a porter to help him gently lift the precious cargo on to a trolley and it was like this, with Crowley preceding sternly in his top hat and cane, that the unlikely procession made its way to a waiting cab. Pulling away from the kerb, Crowley closed the glass partition loudly shut as the driver tried to engage him in conversation. The rest of their journey was undertaken in a brittle silence.

Nearing Boleskine, Crowley held firmly to the large bundle while the car slowly traversed the gravel drive and came to a stop at the front door. Once inside and finally alone, he began to remove the packing tape and velvet with the careful precision of a trained surgeon.

His prize sparkled as it revealed itself in the light that came streaming through the open curtains.

The gilt frame was just as he remembered, etched with inlaid crosses and Zoroastrian triangles, the two pillars, Boaz on the left and Jachin on the right, guardians of the divine gateway.

The glass itself was said to be backed not with mercury but meteorite, forged in some cosmic furnace and sent crashing to earth from the angry stars above.

The base of the frame bore Yeats' later addition 'DEDI', but Yeats had no more of a claim to the Looking Glass than Mathers. For what right had Yeats, Mathers, or any other man to deny Crowley his true destiny?

Now with the Looking Glass in his possession he could dedicate himself solely to the 'The Great Operation', a Magickal ceremony that would reveal everything humanity had strived for but failed to understand: to achieve mystical communion with the Godhead and live on forever as an immortal.

Chapter Four

Alice hurried on in the dimming light and upon turning a corner came upon two fat little men standing stone-still beneath an oak tree. Without any doubt she felt sure that they must be Tweedledee and Tweedledum. Each had an arm around the other's shoulder and it was pretty obvious which was which, as one had DUM embroidered on his collar and the other DEE. But although Alice felt sure she could see their chests rise out so slightly, they were both standing as still as statues in a museum.

In fact, they were so still that Alice wasn't sure that they were alive at all and she was just walking around the back of them to check whether the word Tweedle was on either of their shirt collars when a high pitched voice squeaked out from the one marked DUM.

'If you think we're waxworks,' he said, 'you ought to pay, you know. Waxworks weren't made to be looked at for nothing. No-how!'

'Contrariwise,' added the one marked DEE, 'if you think we're alive you ought to speak.'

'I don't think you're waxworks; it's just that you were standing very still.'

As she was saying this, Alice couldn't help but think of the words of an old nursery rhyme that her grandmother used to sing:

> *'Tweedledum and Tweedledee,*
> *Agreed to have a battle:*
> *For Tweedledum said Tweedledee*
> *Had spoiled his nice new rattle.*
>
> *Just then flew down a monstrous crow,*
> *As black as a tar barrel;*
> *Which frightened both the heroes so,*
> *They quite forgot their quarrel."*

'I know what you're thinking about,' said Tweedledum, 'but it isn't so, nohow.'

'Contrariwise,' continued Tweedledum, 'if it was so, it might still be; and if it were so, it would be; but as it isn't, it ain't. That's logic.'

'I was thinking,' said Alice politely, 'whether you gentlemen might be able to tell me the best way out of this wood as it's getting rather late.' This was not what Alice had been thinking about but it was what she was thinking about right now.

She found these two identical little men quite unsettling. It wasn't just the odd way that they spoke but also the fact they had been standing so still, waiting out here in the middle of nowhere or no-name or whatever this wood was called and for what?

But instead of answering they only looked at each other and grinned. The way they were dressed was weird too, like public schoolboys in their caps and school uniforms but surely they couldn't have been to school for years. They were grown men.

40

Alice repeated her question, only louder this time.

'Nohow!' Tweedledum instantly responded and snapped his mouth shut like a trap.

'How about you? Do you think you could tell me?' said Alice looking at Tweedledee, though as seemed to be the pattern he only shouted out, 'Contrariwise.'

'You've begun wrong!' cried Tweedledum. 'The first thing in a visit is to say "How d'ye do?" and shake hands!' And here the two brothers gave each other a hug and held out two hands to shake hands with her.

Alice didn't know whose hand to shake first as she didn't want to offend either one of them so she took both of their hands at once and the next moment they were dancing round in a ring.

Things were so extraordinary in this world that she was no longer surprised to find she could hear music start up. It seemed to be coming from a nearby tree, whose branches rubbed across each other like bows on violin strings. Alice usually quite liked dancing, however the other two dancers were out of condition and soon out of breath.

'Four times round is enough for one dance,' Tweedledum panted, and they broke off from dancing as quickly as they had begun.

Then they let go of Alice's hands and stood looking at her. This new pause lasted for what seemed like a long time and after a while Alice wanted to say something just to fill up the silence. But she didn't want to say 'How d'ye do?' Not only did it sound silly but as they had just been dancing together, they seemed to have gone beyond such formalities.

'I hope that dancing hasn't tired you out,' she said at last.

'Nohow. Thank you very much for asking,' said Tweedledum.

41

'So much obliged!' added Tweedledee. 'What brings you here? Do you seek the Vorpal Sword? Is it true you are going to fight the Jabberwock?'

'Shhh, Tweedledee, contrariwise. Let's talk of poetry instead. Do you like poetry?' enquired Tweedledum.

'Ye-es, well... some poetry,' Alice said rather doubtfully. 'But could you tell me which road leads out of the wood?'

'What shall I repeat to her?' said Tweedledee, looking round at Tweedledum with great solemn eyes whilst completely ignoring Alice's question.

'The Walrus and the Carpenter' is the longest,' Tweedledum replied, giving his brother an affectionate hug, and Tweedledee began instantly:

> *'The sun was shining-'*

Here Alice felt forced to interrupt. 'If it's very long,' she said as politely as she could manage, 'would you first tell me which road -'

But Tweedledee only smiled gently and began again:

> *'The sun was shining on the sea,*
> *He did his very best to make*
> *The billows smooth and bright -*
> *And this was odd, because it was*
> *The middle of the night.*
>
> *The sea was wet as wet could be,*
> *The sands were dry as dry.*
> *You could not see a cloud, because*
> *No cloud was in the sky:*
> *No birds were flying overhead-*
> *There were no birds to fly.*

The Walrus and the Carpenter
    Were walking hand in hand:
They wept like anything to see
    Such quantities of sand:
'If this were only cleared away,'
    They said, 'it would be grand!'

'O Oysters, come and walk with us!'
    The Walrus did beseech.
'A pleasant walk, a pleasant talk,
    Along the briny beach:
We cannot do with more than four.
    To give a hand to each.'

The eldest Oyster looked at him,
    But never a word he said:
The eldest Oyster winked his eye,
    And shook his heavy head -
Meaning to say he did not choose
    To leave the oyster-bed.

But four young Oysters hurried up,
    All eager for the treat:
Their coats were brushed, their faces washed,
    Their shoes were clean and neat-
And this was odd, because, you know,
    They hadn't any feet.

Four other Oysters followed them,
    And yet another four:
And thick and fast they came at last,
    And more, and more, and more-
All hopping through the frothy waves,
    And scrambling to the shore.

The Walrus and the Carpenter
    Walked on a mile or so,
And then they rested on a rock
    Conveniently low:
And all the little Oysters stood
    And waited in a row.

'The time has come,' the Walrus said,
    'To talk of many things:
Of shoes-and ships-and sealing wax-
    Of cabbages-and kings-
And why the sea is boiling hot-
    And whether pigs have wings.'

'A loaf of bread,' the Walrus said,
    'Is what we chiefly need:
Pepper and vinegar besides
    Are very good indeed-
Now, if you're ready, Oysters dear,
    We can begin to feed.'

'But not on us!' the Oysters cried,
  Turning a little blue.
'After such kindness, that would be
  A dismal thing to do!'
'The night is fine,' the Walrus said.
  'Do you admire the view?

'It was so kind of you to come!
  And you are very nice!'
The Carpenter said nothing but
  'Cut us another slice.
I wish you were not quite so deaf-
  I've had to ask you twice!'

'It seems a shame,' the Walrus said:
  'To play them such a trick.
After we've brought them out so far,
  And made them trot so quick!'
The Carpenter said nothing but
  'The butter's spread too thick!'

'I weep for you,' the Walrus said:
  'I deeply sympathize.'
With sobs and tears he sorted out
  Those of the largest size,
Holding his pocket-handkerchief
  Before his streaming eyes.

'O Oysters,' said the Carpenter,
  'You've had a pleasant run!
Shall we be trotting home again?'
  But answer came there none-
And this was scarcely odd, because
  They'd eaten every one.'

'What a horrible poem,' said Alice, 'but I suppose at least the Walrus felt sorry for the Oysters.'

'He ate more than the Carpenter though,' said Tweedledee. 'You see, he held his handkerchief in front so that the Carpenter couldn't count how many he took: contrariwise.'

'Then I prefer the Carpenter if he ate less than the Walrus.'

'Ah, but he ate as many as he could get,' said Tweedledum.

'Well, it's obvious that they were both very nasty types of people who were not worth writing a poem about!'

'Contrariwise, would you like to see a sight that is worth writing about?' asked Tweedledum.

'Is it on the way out of this place?' said Alice, suddenly more interested.

'Yes, come and look!' the brothers cried and they each took one of Alice's hands and led her to a clearing in the centre of which stood a large dome-shaped tent. It was far grander and more elegant than any tent Alice had ever seen before. An embroidered rampant lion stared out defiantly above its entrance with the words *Deo duce comite ferro* below, the roof was edged with a sparkling jewelled hem and even the drawstrings had silk tassels.

'Wow! That's a posh tent,' exclaimed Alice.

'Contrariwise, it's the Royal Field Tent and the White King sleeps inside,' said Tweedledum beckoning her forward.

The three of them entered the tent in a respectful silence. It was dark and the warm air hung heavy with the bitter-sweet smell of incense. In contrast to the grandiosity of the exterior, a simple wooden bed was visible on their opposite side and on it lay the figure of a man dressed only in a long cotton night shirt.

'Isn't he a lovely sight?' said Tweedledum.

Alice couldn't honestly say that he was. His shirt had been stained dark in patches and though sleeping, his sleep was fevered and the dreams that he could see caused him to twitch and mumble. As Alice got closer she could feel the heat rise from his body and warm her skin.

'He's very sick. Does he not have a doctor? Someone needs to help him.'

'No need for that, come outside and I'll explain it there,' said Tweedledee.

Once back outside Tweedledee fixed Alice with a menacing stare.

'The King is dreaming now,' he said 'and what do you think he dreams about?'

'I honestly don't know,' replied Alice.

'Why, he's dreaming about you!' Tweedledee exclaimed, clapping his hands together triumphantly. 'And if he stopped dreaming about you, where do you suppose you'd be?'

'Here, where I am now of course,' said Alice.

'Not you, you're a no-one,' Tweedledee retorted contemptuously, 'and you'd be nowhere. Why you're only a sort of thing in one of his dreams!'

'If that there King was to wake,' added Tweedledum, 'you'd go out – bang!- just like a light!'

'I wouldn't!' Alice exclaimed indignantly. 'Besides, if I'm only a thing in one of his dreams, what does that make you?'

'Ditto,' said Tweedledum.

'Ditto, ditto!' cried Tweedledee.

He shouted this so loud that Alice politely asked if he could please stop making such a racket.

'Why? Don't you like tennis? We might play real tennis if you were real but as you're not, it's no surprise that you don't like a racquet.'

'I am real and I'm getting really quite annoyed,' and with this she kicked Tweedledee sharply on his left shin.

'Ouch!' cried Tweedledee, hopping about on his right foot. 'There was no need to do that!'

'But if I'm not real then it doesn't really matter because that wasn't a real kick. I'm sorry if it hurt but I was only trying to test your theory. Now I'd better be making my way out of the wood because it's getting a bit dark. Do you think it's going to rain?'

Tweedledum spread a large umbrella over himself and his brother and looked up into it.

'No, I don't think so,' he said, 'at least - not under here.'

'But do you think it might rain where I am?'

'It might if it chooses,' said Tweedledee: 'we've no objection. Contrariwise.'

'Selfish twits!' thought Alice. She was just about to say 'Good-bye' and leave them when Tweedledum sprang out from under the umbrella and seized her by the wrist.

'Do you see that?' he said in a voice choking with anger. His eyes grew large and yellow all in a moment as he pointed his trembling finger at a white thing lying under the tree.

Alice bent down and took a look at the small white object that seemed to be the cause of the fuss.

'What's the matter with you? It's only a rattle, not a rattle-snake,' she said, thinking he was somehow frightened of it. 'Just a rattle, quite old and rather broken.'

'I knew it was!' cried Tweedledum, beginning to stamp about wildly and tear at his hair. 'It's spoilt of course!' He looked ma-levolently at Tweedledee who immediately sat down on the ground and tried to hide himself under the umbrella.

'There's no need to get so upset about an old rattle,' said Alice in a soothing tone.

'But it isn't old!' Tweedledum cried, in a greater fury than ever. 'It's new I tell you - I bought it yesterday - my nice new RAT-TLE!' and brought his voice to a perfect scream.

All this time Tweedledee was trying his best to fold up the umbrella with himself still in it which was such a strange procedure that it distracted Alice's attention from his angry brother. But Tweedledee couldn't quite succeed in the task and it ended up with him rolling over, bundled up in the umbrella with only his head sticking out and there he lay, opening and shutting his mouth and his large eyes.

'He looks more like a very silly fish than anything else,' thought Alice.

'Of course you agree to have a battle?' Tweedledum said in a calmer tone.

'I suppose so,' the other brother sulkily replied, as he crawled out of the umbrella.

'There's only one sword you know,' said Tweedledum, 'but you can have the umbrella. It's nearly as sharp. Only we must begin quickly. It's getting as dark as it can.'
'And darker,' said Tweedledee.

It was getting dark so suddenly that Alice thought there must be a thunderstorm coming on. 'What a thick black cloud that is!' she said, 'and how fast it's moving. It's kind of like it's got wings!'

'That's the crow!' Tweedledum cried out in a shrill voice of alarm and the two brothers took to their heels and were gone without another word.

Alice ran a little way into the wood and stopped under a large tree. 'It'll never get me here,' she told herself, "that thing's far too big to squeeze down amongst these trees but its wings are flapping so hard it's making some sort of hurricane – and here's somebody's shawl that's blown away!'

Boleskine House, Foyers, Scottish Highlands

The night had been punctuated by violent storms and now in the stillness of dawn, Crowley could not shake the feeling that something was amiss. It was not simply quiet, there was complete silence. No wind, no birdsong… and not a sound from his dogs…

Where were his dogs?

Crowley leapt from his bed with an athleticism that belied his size and crashed out of the door in just gown and sandals. He whistled and called out loud but there was no response.

Skirting around the back of the house he yelled and whistled louder, yet still there was nothing. Moving more quickly now, up towards the woodland, there in the bracken he could see a dark shape. As he approached nearer, the object began to materialise. The outline sharpened until he could see it was clearly the body of an animal, his alpha dog, the one he called Sirius.

Crowley bent down in the wet grass and examined the scene more closely. The corpse was stiff with legs outstretched as though frozen in flight, jaws open in a snarl but without any external signs of injury. This didn't seem like the work of any natural predator. Crowley looked for traces of vomit on its coat as even a poison would leave symptoms but here

51

again there was nothing. Then he remembered the words of an oath he had once given: 'If I break this Magical obligation I might fall slain and paralysed without visible weapon as if slain by the lightning flash.'

It would seem that Mathers had found him.

Chapter Five

Alice caught the shawl as she spoke and looked around the trees for its owner.

In another moment the White Queen came running through the wood, with both arms stretched out wide as if she were flying and Alice very civilly went to meet her with the shawl.

'I'm glad I happened to be in the way,' said Alice as she handed her the shawl to put back on.

The White Queen only looked at her in a helpless frightened sort of way, and kept whispering something that sounded like 'Bread-and-butter, bread-and butter'. Alice felt that if there was going to be any conversation at all she had better start it herself. So she began by simply asking, 'Am I addressing the White Queen?'

'Well, yes if you can call that a-dressing,' the Queen replied. 'It isn't my notion of the thing.'

Alice thought it a bad idea to argue the point so she smiled and said, 'If your Majesty can tell me the right way to begin, then I'll do it as well as I can.'

'But I don't want it done at all!' groaned the Queen. 'I've been a-dressing myself for the past two hours.'

It seemed to Alice that it actually might have been better to get someone else to dress her as she hadn't made a great job of it on her own

'Every single thing's crooked,' Alice thought to herself. 'May I help get your shawl a little more straight for you?' she added aloud.

'I don't know what's the matter with it!' the Queen said in a melancholy voice. 'I think it's in a temper. I've pinned it here and I've pinned it there but there's no pleasing it!'

'It can't go straight you know, if you pin it all on one side,' Alice said, as she gently put it right for her. 'And your hair's in a bit of a state. Let me see what I can do.'

'The hairbrush has got entangled in it!' the Queen said with a sigh, 'and I lost the comb yesterday.'

Alice carefully released the brush and did her best to get the Queen's hair into some sort of order. 'That's much better now,' she said, after altering most of the hairpins. 'But you should think about getting a lady's-maid.'

'I'm sure I'll take you with pleasure!' the Queen said, 'two pounds a week and jam every other day.'

Alice couldn't help laughing, as she said, 'I don't want you to hire me - and I don't care for jam.'

'It's very good jam,' said the Queen.

'Well, I don't want any today at any rate.'

'You couldn't have it even if you did want it,' the Queen replied. 'The rule is jam tomorrow and jam yesterday but never jam today.'

'It must sometimes come to jam today,' Alice objected.

'No, it can't,' said the Queen. 'It's jam every other day; today isn't any other day you know.'

'I don't really understand what you mean. It's quite confusing,'

'That's the effect of living backwards,' the Queen said kindly. 'It always makes one a little giddy at first.'

'Living backwards!' Alice repeated in astonishment.

'But the one great advantage to it is one's memory works both ways.'

'I'm sure mine only works one way,' said Alice, 'when it works at all.'

'It's a very poor sort of memory that only works backwards,' the Queen remarked.

'What sort of things do you remember best?' Alice ventured.

'Oh, things that happened the week after next,' the Queen replied nonchalantly. 'For instance,' she went on, sticking a large piece of plaster on her finger as she spoke, 'there's the King's

Messenger. He's in prison now, being punished and the trial doesn't even begin till next Wednesday and of course the crime comes last of all.'

'But suppose he never commits the crime?' said Alice.

'That would be all the better, wouldn't it?' the Queen said, as she bound the plaster round her finger with a bit of ribbon.

There was no denying that.

'Of course it would be all the better,' Alice said, 'but it wouldn't be all the better him being punished for it.'

'You're wrong there, at any rate,' said the Queen. 'Were you ever punished?'

'Only once,' said Alice. 'It was when I was younger and I went off on my own without telling anyone, I wasn't allowed out for a while after that.'

'Ha! and you were all the better for it, I know!' said the Queen triumphantly.

'But I had done the thing I was punished for,' said Alice 'and that makes all the difference.'

'But if you hadn't done it,' the Queen said, 'that would be better still, better, and better and better!'

Her voice went higher with each 'better' till it got to quite a squeak at last.

Alice was just beginning to say, 'There's a mistake somewhere--,' when the Queen began screaming so loud that she had to leave the sentence unfinished.

'Oh, oh, oh!' shouted the Queen, shaking her hand about as if she wanted to shake it off. 'My finger's bleeding! Oh, oh, oh, oh!'

Her screams were beginning to sound so much like the shriek of a car alarm that Alice had to hold both her hands over her ears.

'What's the matter?' asked Alice, as soon as there was a chance of making herself heard. 'Have you pricked your finger?'

'I haven't pricked it yet,' the Queen said, 'but I soon shall - oh, oh, oh!'

'When do you expect to do that?' said Alice, finding it difficult not to laugh.

'When I fasten my shawl again,' the poor Queen groaned out, 'the brooch will come undone directly. Oh oh!' As she said the words the brooch flew open and the Queen clutched wildly at it and tried to clasp it again.

'Be careful!' cried Alice. 'You're holding it all crooked!' and she caught the brooch but it was too late: the pin had slipped and the Queen had pricked her finger.

'That accounts for the bleeding, you see,' she said to Alice with a smile. 'Now you understand the way things happen here.'

'But why are you not screaming now?' Alice asked, holding her hands ready to put over her ears again.

'Why I've done all the screaming already,' said the Queen. 'What would be the good of having it all over again?'

By this time it was getting light.

'I think the crow must have flown away,' said Alice. 'I'm so glad it's gone. I thought it was night closing in.'

'I wish I could manage to be glad!' the Queen said. 'Only I never can remember the rule. You must be very happy living in the wood and being glad whenever you like.'

But Alice wasn't feeling very happy, she was thinking about her father.

'It's very lonely here!' Alice said in a melancholy voice and with this sudden realisation, two large tears came rolling down her cheeks. Alice wiped them away with her cuff hoping that the

Queen wouldn't notice.

'Oh, don't go on like that!' cried the Queen, wringing her hands in despair. 'Consider what a great girl you are. Consider what a long way you've come today. Consider what o'clock it is. Consider anything, but don't cry!'

Alice could not help laughing at this, even in the midst of her tears.

'Can you keep from crying by considering things?' she asked.

'That's the way it's done,' the Queen said with great decision. 'Nobody can do two things at once, you know. Let's consider your age to begin with. How old are you?'

'Thirteen and a bit, I don't remember exactly,' replied Alice.

'You needn't say exactly,' the Queen remarked. 'I can believe it without that. Now I'll give you something to believe. I'm just one hundred and eleven years, five months and a day.'

'I can't believe that!' said Alice.

'Can't you?' the Queen said in a pitying tone.' Try again; draw a long breath and shut your eyes.'

Alice laughed. 'There's no use trying,' she said, 'I can't believe impossible things.'

'I dare say you haven't had much practice,' said the Queen. 'When I was your age, I always did it for half an hour a day. Why, sometimes I believed as many as six impossible things before breakfast. Oh no, there goes the shawl again!'

The brooch had come undone as she spoke and a sudden gust of wind blew her shawl across a little brook. The Queen spread her arms out like an aeroplane and went flying after it and this time succeeded in catching it by herself.

'I've got it!' she cried in a triumphant tone. 'Now you shall see me pin it on again, all by myself!'

'Then I hope your finger feels better now,' Alice said very politely as she crossed the little brook after the Queen.

'Oh, much better!' cried the Queen, her voice rising into a squeak as she went on. 'Much be-etter! Be-etter! Much Be-etter! Be-e-e-etter! Be-e-ehh!'

The last word ended in a long bleat, so like a sheep that it startled Alice. She looked at the Queen who seemed to have suddenly wrapped herself up in wool. Alice rubbed her eyes and looked again. She couldn't make out what had happened at all. Was she in some kind of shop? And was that really - was it really a sheep that was sitting behind the counter? Try as she might, she could make no more of it: she was in a small dark shop and opposite her sitting in an armchair behind the counter sat an old sheep.

'What is it that you want to buy?' the Sheep asked, surveying Alice through some large spectacles.

'I don't quite know yet,' said Alice very gently.' I'd like to look all around first if that's all right.'

'You may look in front of you and on both sides,' said the Sheep, 'but you can't look all around you - unless you've got eyes at the back of your head.'

But Alice did not have eyes there so she contented herself with turning around and looking in her usual way. The interior was shelved in bright glass and dark wood with rows of tinted bottles lining the shelves like an old fashioned apothecary shop. The bottles had large stoppers and attractive labels with handwritten script to identify their contents. On the nearest shelf was one which read Tonic of Zinc and Goldenseal.

'That's interesting,' thought Alice, and reached out to pick it up but just as her fingers were virtually touching the bottle, it vanished into thin air. Undaunted, she continued along the shelves until her eyes alighted on the most beautiful bottle she had ever seen.

The glass was a midnight blue colour but looked almost purple from some angles and was shaped as sensually as the curves of a heart. It had been labelled with a flourish and read Essence of a Black Rose.

'How lovely, I wonder if it's perfume?' said Alice but this time as she reached for it, the bottle gently lifted into the air and continued up through the ceiling until it disappeared from her sight.

'Essence of a black rose,' said Alice under her breath. 'Well, they weren't wrong about that; it rose right up through the roof!'

'Are you going to buy something or just carry on looking around?' asked the Sheep. 'You'll only make yourself dizzy like that.'

'Well it's not easy to choose because everything I want to buy keeps disappearing,' said Alice in a tone of slight frustration.

'Oh, that's because of the Red Queen's decree,' explained the Sheep. 'Our traditional medicines couldn't cure the King so this shop has been officially declared to be By Royal Dis-appointment. We are not allowed to sell real things any more, only the idea of them. What you see on the shelves are just your ideas of things.'

'How confusing,' remarked Alice.

'It was the same with the farms, she got so angry with the farmers that she cancelled all the cereals!'

'Why did she do that?' asked Alice. 'Is she gluten intolerant?'

'Oh yes, I should think so,' said the Sheep, 'she's not a very tolerant type of person!'

'Are you allowed to sell anything real?'

'Only eggs.'

'Well in that case, I would like to buy an egg.'

'They're fifty pennies each,' replied the Sheep.

'Then I'll have one please' said Alice putting the money down on the counter.

The Sheep took the money and put it away in a box. Then she said, 'I never put things into people's hands - that would never do – you must get it for yourself.' And so saying, she went off to the other end of the shop and set the egg upright on a shelf.

'I wonder why it wouldn't do?' thought Alice as she groped her way among the tables and chairs for it was very dark at the back of the shop.

'This egg seems to get further away the more I walk towards it. Let me see, is this a chair? Hang on, it's got branches! There are actually trees growing in here! And now there's another one of these little brooks. This is the oddest shop I've ever been in!'

Despite all this Alice carried on, with each object turning into a tree as she drew near to it. She was quite sure the egg would do the same.

Montmartre
Paris

With every day that passed the same journey was becoming harder for him. Mathers had almost reached the end of the Rue St. Vincent before deciding to turn back. He could hide the truth from everyone but himself and the truth was that he was dying.

'An unusual predicament,' thought Mathers, 'to know in advance the exact year and month of one's demise and yet have only one chance to avoid it.' He was accepting of the fact, but with his bloodline hunted to near extinction, finding a successor had proven difficult, almost impossible. There would be objections from certain quarters, but the tradition of a male heir was by no means sacrosanct. What worried him more was that he had been forced to choose someone so young and ill-prepared.

A serious problem indeed, but it would have to wait as he was going to need to conserve all his energies for the evening ahead. Under-estimating Mr Aleister Crowley was not a mistake he could afford to make twice, for in attempting to know the unknowable, Crowley was tampering with forces powerful enough to destroy all humanity. His previous attempt on Crowley's Scottish powerbase had proved deadly only to his dogs, the man himself survived unscathed. If anything he was becoming stronger. Mathers had no choice but to play his final card, a spell so dangerous that he had censored it from all his books and teachings. Tonight he would invoke the demons of Abra-Melin to hunt down Crowley in his chamber at Boleskine and tear him from this world of men. If successful, Crowley would live on only as a shadow, a dim reflection of his own twisted ambitions, enslaved within the very Looking Glass he had sought to make him king.

Chapter Six

As Alice approached nearer, instead of turning into a tree, the egg only got larger and larger and more and more human. When she had come within a few yards of it, she saw that it had eyes and a nose and mouth and when she got even closer, she saw quite clearly that it was Humpty Dumpty himself.

'It can't be anybody else!' she said to herself. 'It's as plain as if his name were written all over his face!'

It might have been written a hundred times, easily, on that enormous face. Humpty Dumpty was sitting with his legs crossed, like a Buddha, on top of a high wall – such a narrow one that Alice was surprised he could keep his balance – and, as his eyes were steadily fixed in the opposite direction and he didn't take any notice of her, she thought he must be a stuffed figure after all.

'And how exactly like an egg he is!' she said aloud, standing with her hands ready to catch him, for she was expecting him to fall at any moment.

'It's very provoking,' Humpty Dumpty said after a long silence, looking away from Alice as he spoke, 'to be called an egg – very!'

'I said you looked like an egg,' Alice explained. 'And some eggs are very pretty, you know, like Easter eggs or Fabergé eggs,' she added, hoping to turn her remark into a sort of compliment.

'Some people,' said Humpty Dumpty, looking away from her, 'have no more sense than a baby!'

Alice didn't know what to say to this: it wasn't like a normal conversation at all, she thought, as he never said anything to her; in fact, his last remark was evidently addressed to a tree – so she stood and recited softly to herself -

> *'Humpty Dumpty sat on a wall:*
> *Humpty Dumpty had a great fall.*
> *All the King's horses and all the King's men*
> *Couldn't put Humpty back together again.'*

She spoke the last line almost out loud, forgetting Humpty Dumpty might hear her.

'Don't stand chattering to yourself like that,' Humpty Dumpty said, looking at her for the first time, 'but tell me your name and your business.'

'My name is Alice, but -'

'It's a stupid name enough!' Humpty Dumpty interrupted impatiently. 'What does it mean?'

'Must a name mean something?' Alice asked doubtfully.

'Of course it must,' Humpty Dumpty said with a short laugh. 'My name means the shape I am – and a good handsome shape it is, too. With a name like yours, you might be any shape, almost.'

'Why are you sitting out here all alone?' said Alice, not wishing to start an argument.

'Why, because there's nobody with me!' cried Humpty Dumpty.

'Did you think I didn't know the answer to that? Ask another.'

'Don't you think you'd be safer down on the ground?' Alice went on, not with the intention of making another riddle, but simply in her good-natured concern for the strange creature's safety. 'That wall is very narrow!'

'What tremendously easy riddles you ask!' Humpty Dumpty cried out. 'Of course I don't think so! Why, if ever I did fall off – which there's no chance of – but if I did -'

Here he pursed up his lips and looked so solemn and grand that Alice could hardly help laughing. 'If I did fall,' he went on, 'the King has promised me – ah, you may turn pale, if you like! You didn't think I was going to say that, did you? The King has promised me with his own mouth – to – to -'

'To send all his horses and all of his men,' Alice interrupted, rather unwisely.

'Now I declare that's too bad!' Humpty Dumpty cried, breaking into a sudden temper. 'You've been listening at doors – and behind trees – and down chimneys – or you couldn't have known it!'

'I have not,' said Alice very gently. 'It was in a book I read.'

'Ah, well! They may write such things in a book,' Humpty Dumpty said in a calmer tone. 'That's what you call a History book, that is. Now, take a good look at me! I'm one that has spoken to a King, I am. Mayhap you'll never see such another and to show you I'm not proud, you may shake hands with me!' And he grinned almost from ear to ear, as he leant forwards (nearly falling off the wall in doing so) and offered Alice his hand.

She watched him a little anxiously as she took it.

'If he smiled much more, the ends of his mouth might meet behind,' she thought, 'and then I don't know what would happen to his head! I'm worried it might fall off!'

'Yes, all his horses and all his men,' Humpty Dumpty went on. 'They'd pick me up again in a minute, they would! However this conversation is going on a little too fast, let's go back to the last remark but one.'

'I'm afraid I don't quite remember it,' replied Alice very politely.

'In that case we may start afresh,' said Humpty Dumpty, 'and it's my turn to choose a subject, so here's a question for you. How old did you say you were?'

Alice made a quick calculation and said, 'Thirteen years and almost six months.'

'Wrong!' Humpty Dumpty exclaimed triumphantly. 'You never said a word like it.'

'I thought you meant, "How old are you?"' Alice explained.

'If I'd meant that, I'd have said it,' said Humpty Dumpty. Alice didn't want another argument so she said nothing.

'Thirteen years and six months!' Humpty Dumpty repeated slowly. 'An uncomfortable sort of age. Now if you'd asked my advice, I'd have said "Leave off at thirteen" - but it's too late now.'

'I've never asked anyone's advice about growing up,' Alice said rather indignantly.

'Too proud?' the other enquired.

She felt even more indignant at this suggestion. 'I mean,' said Alice, 'that one can't help growing older.'

'One can't, perhaps,' said Humpty Dumpty rather menacingly, 'but two can. With proper assistance, you might have left off at thirteen.'

'What a beautiful belt you've got on!' Alice suddenly remarked in an effort to change the subject. 'At least,' she corrected herself on second thoughts, 'a beautiful cravat, I should have said – no, a belt, I mean – oh, I beg your pardon!' she added in dismay, for Humpty Dumpty looked thoroughly offended, and she began to wish she hadn't chosen this particular diversion. 'If only I knew,' she thought to herself, 'which was neck and which was waist!'

Evidently Humpty Dumpty was very angry, though he said nothing for a minute or two. When he did speak again, it was in a deep growl.

'It is a – most – provoking- thing,' he said at last, 'when a person doesn't know a cravat from a belt!'

'I know it really is quite ignorant of me,' Alice replied in so humble a voice that Humpty Dumpty relented.

'It's a cravat, child, and a beautiful one, as you say. It's a present from the White King and Queen. There now!'

'Is it really?' said Alice, quite pleased to find she had chosen a good subject, after all.

'They gave it to me,' Humpty Dumpty continued thoughtfully, as he crossed one knee over the other and clasped his hands round it, ' - for an un-birthday present.'

'I'm sorry?' Alice said with a puzzled air.

'What for? I'm not offended,' said Humpty Dumpty.

'I mean, what is an un-birthday present?'

'A present given when it isn't your birthday, of course.'

Alice considered this a little. 'I think I like birthday presents best,' she said at last.

'You don't know what you're talking about!' cried Humpty Dumpty. ' How many days are there in a year?'

'Three hundred and sixty-five,' said Alice.

'And how many birthdays have you?'

'One.'

'And if you take one from three hundred and sixty-five, what remains?'

'Three hundred and sixty-four, of course.'

Humpty Dumpty looked doubtful. 'I'd rather see that done on paper,' he said.

$$365$$
$$-1$$
$$= 364$$

Alice couldn't help smiling as she took out her note-book, and wrote the sum down for him:

Humpty Dumpty took the book and looked at it very carefully. 'That seems to be done right,' he began.

'You're holding it upside down!' Alice interrupted.

'To be sure I was!' Humpty Dumpty said gaily, as she turned it round for him. 'I thought it looked a little unusual. As I was saying, that seems to be done right – though I haven't time to look it over thoroughly just now – and that shows that there are three hundred and sixty-four days when you might get un-birthday presents -'

'Certainly,' said Alice.

'And only one for birthday presents, you know. There's glory for you!'

'Glory ? I don't really know what you're on about,' said Alice.

Humpty Dumpty smiled contemptuously. 'Of course you don't – till I tell you. I meant "there's a nice knockdown argument for you!"

'But "glory" doesn't mean "a nice knockdown argument", objected Alice.

'When I use a word,' Humpty Dumpty said in rather a scornful tone, 'it means just what I choose it to mean – neither more nor less.'

'The question is,' said Alice, 'whether you can make words mean different things.'

'The question is,' said Humpty Dumpty, 'which is to be master – that's all.'

Alice was too puzzled to say anything so after a minute Humpty Dumpty began again. 'They've a temper some of them – particularly verbs, they're the proudest. Adjectives you can do anything with but not verbs – however I can manage the whole lot! Impenetrability! That's what I say!'

'Would you tell me, please,' said Alice, 'what that means?'

'Now you talk like a reasonable child,' said Humpty Dumpty, looking very much pleased. 'I meant by "impenetrability" that we've had enough of that subject and it would be just as well if you'd mention what you mean to do next, as I suppose you don't intend to stop here all the rest of your life.'

'That's a great deal to make one word mean,' said Alice thoughtfully.

'When I make a word do a lot of work like that,' said Humpty Dumpty, 'I always pay it extra.'

'Oh right,' said Alice. She had intended to ask him if he knew where to find the Vorpal sword but now decided any answer he gave would only leave her more confused.

'Ah, you should see 'em come round me of a Saturday night,' Humpty Dumpty went on, wagging his head gravely from side to side, 'to get their wages, you know.'

'You seem very clever at explaining words,' said Alice. 'Would you kindly tell me the meaning of the poem "Jabberwocky"?'

'Let's hear it,' said Humpty Dumpty. 'I can explain all the poems that were ever invented – and a good many that haven't been invented just yet.'

This sounded very hopeful so Alice repeated the first verse:

'*Twas brillig, and the slithy toves*
Did gyre and gimble in the wabe:
All mimsy were the borogroves,
And the mome raths outgrabe.'

'That's enough to begin with,' Humpty Dumpty interrupted. 'There are plenty of hard words there. "Brillig" means four o'clock in the afternoon – the time when you begin broiling things for dinner.'

'That makes sense,' said Alice, 'and "slithy"?'

'Well, "slithy" means "lithe and slimy". "Lithe" is the same as "active". You see it's like a portmanteau - there are two meanings packed up into one word.'

'I can see that now,' Alice remarked thoughtfully, ' and what are "toves"?'

'Well, "toves" are something like badgers – they're something like lizards – and they're something like corkscrews.'

'They must be very unusual creatures.'

'They are that,' said Humpty Dumpty, 'also they make their nests under sundials – also they live on cheese.'

'And what's to "gyre" and to "gimble"?'

'To "gyre" is to go round and round like a gyroscope. To "gimble" is to make holes like a gimlet.'

'And "the wabe" is the grass plot round a sundial, I suppose?' said Alice, surprised at her own ingenuity.

'Of course it is. It's called "wabe", you know, because it goes a long way before it, and a long way behind it -'

'And a long way beyond it on each side,' Alice added.

'Exactly so. Well then, "mimsy" is "flimsy and miserable" (there's another portmanteau for you). And a "borogrove" is a thin shabby-looking bird with its feathers sticking out all round – something like a live mop.'

'And then "mome raths"?' said Alice.' If I'm not giving you too much trouble.'

'Well, a "rath" is a sort of green pig but "mome" I'm not certain about. I think it's short for "from home" - meaning that they'd lost their way, you know.'

'And what does "outgrabe" mean?'

'Well, "outgrabing" is something between bellowing and whistling, with a nasty kind of sneeze in the middle. However, you'll hear it done, maybe – down in the wood yonder – and when you've once heard it you'll not forget it. Who's been repeating all this hard stuff to you?'

'I read it in a book,' said Alice. 'But I had some much easier poetry repeated to me by – Tweedledee, I think.'

'As to poetry, you know,' said Humpty Dumpty, stretching out one of his great hands, ' I can repeat poetry as well as other folk if it comes to that.'

'Oh, it needn't come to that!' Alice hastily said, hoping to keep him from beginning.

'The piece I'm going to repeat,' he went on without noticing her remark, 'was written entirely for your amusement.'

Alice felt that in that case she really ought to listen to it, so she sat down, and said, 'Thank you,' rather resignedly.

> *'In winter, when the fields are white,*
> *I sing this song for your delight-*

only I don't sing it,' he explained.

'I see you don't,' said Alice.

'If you can see whether I'm singing or not, you've sharper eyes than most,' Humpty Dumpty remarked severely. Alice was silent.

> *In spring, when woods are getting green,*
> *I'll try and tell you what I mean.'*

'Thank you very much,' said Alice.

> *In summer, when the days are long,*
> *Perhaps you'll understand the song:*

In autumn, when the leaves are brown,
Take a pen and write it down.'

'I will, if I can remember it that long,' said Alice.
'You needn't go on making remarks like that,' Humpty Dumpty said, 'they're not sensible, and they put me out.'

I sent a message to the fish:
I told them, "This is what I wish."

The little fishes of the sea,
They sent an answer back to me.

The little fishes' answer was
"We cannot do it, sir, because -"

'I'm afraid I don't quite understand,' said Alice.
'It gets easier further on,' Humpty Dumpty replied.

'I sent to them again to say
"It will be better to obey."

The fishes answered with a grin,
"Why, what a temper you are in!"

I told them once, I told them twice:
They would not listen to advice.

I took a kettle large and new,
Fit for the deed I had to do.

Then someone came to me and said,
"The little fishes are in bed."

I said to him, I said it plain,
"Then you must wake them up again."

I said it very loud and clear;
I went and shouted in his ear.'

Humpty Dumpty raised his voice almost to a scream as he repeated this verse.

'But he was very stiff and proud;
He said, "You needn't shout so loud!"

And he was very proud and stiff;
He said, "I'd go and wake them, if -"

I took a corkscrew from the shelf:
I went to wake them up myself.

And when I found the door was locked,
I pulled and pushed and kicked and knocked.

And when I found the door was shut
I tried to turn the handle, but -'

There was a long pause. 'Is that all?' asked Alice.

'That's all,' said Humpty Dumpty. 'Goodbye.'

This was rather sudden, Alice thought but after such a very strong hint that she ought to be going, she felt that it would hardly be polite to stay. So she held out her hand.

'Goodbye, till we meet again!' she said as cheerfully as she could.

' I shouldn't know you again if we did meet,' Humpty Dumpty replied in a discontented tone, giving her one of his fingers to shake; 'you're so exactly like other people.'

'The face is what one generally goes by,' Alice remarked thoughtfully.

'That's just what I complain of,' said Humpty Dumpty. 'Your face is the same as everybody else has – the two eyes, like so -' (marking their places in the air with his thumb) 'nose in the middle, mouth under. It's always the same. Now if you had the two eyes on the same side of the nose, for instance - or the mouth at the top – that would be better.'

'It wouldn't look nice,' Alice objected. But Humpty Dumpty only shut his eyes and said, 'Wait till you've tried.'

Alice waited a minute to see if he would speak again, but as he never opened his eyes or took any further notice of her, she said 'Goodbye!' once more, and, on getting no answer, quietly walked away but she couldn't help saying as she went, 'Of all the stubborn people I ever…' but she broke off distracted by a distant rumbling that had started faint but was now getting louder.

Boleskine House, Foyers, Scottish Highlands

The future would be written here at Boleskine, not by a deluded old man clinging hopelessly to past glories. It could have been different had Mathers agreed to share what he knew, but blinded by arrogance and vanity he'd refused and now God had answered.

While he, Crowley was only hours from achieving his life's goal, Mathers was reduced to touting cheap parlour tricks on the filthy streets of Paris.

Boleskine House was perfect both in its architecture and seclusion. Crowley had configured the Temple exactly as laid down by Abra-Melin in *The Book of Sacred Magic* so many centuries ago.

The front door opened onto a terrace that faced north across the loch. Leading back from this was a long hall and along each facing wall he had hung mirrors, their reflections diminishing infinitely in each other's gaze. He had angled the mirrors so that the final pair threw their light onto the one precise spot.

For at the far end of the hall stood the altar and above this was the Looking Glass. Every day the cleansing rituals were observed, then pure Frankincense was set in charcoal burners on the altar and he would kneel and chant the opening lines of The Rite of Saturn as a protection against his former master:

> *Even as the traitor's breath*
> *Goeth forth, he perisheth.*
> *By the secret sibilant word that is spoken unto death,*
> *Even as the profane hand,*
> *Reacheth to the sacred sand,*
> *Fire consumes him, that his name be forgotten in the land.*

Crowley had waited for five moons to rise and fall while preparing for the final conjuration but he need wait no longer for the sixth moon would rise full tonight.

Chapter Seven

The sound steadily grew to a roar and Alice could feel the ground beneath her feet begin to tremble. In the next moment soldiers were running through the wood, their eyes wild with violence and fear.

At first they came in twos and threes, then ten or twenty together and at last in such crowds that they seemed to fill the whole forest. Alice got behind a tree to avoid being trampled as she watched them go by. Then came the horses, their hoof beats drumming out the ancient rhythms of war. The armour of their riders was polished and gleaming so that Alice had to shield her eyes in the moments that it caught sunlight in the gaps between the trees. Relieved when the last of them was finally in the distance, she was able to get out and into an open space. To her surprise, it was here that she found the Red King who was seated on the ground, hastily writing notes into a small book.

'I've sent them all, that's all of them,' he muttered to himself. On seeing Alice he put his pen down and said nervously, 'Hello again my dear, did you happen to see any soldiers, as you came through the wood?'

'Yes I did,' said Alice, 'lots of them actually, several thousand,

I should think.'

'Four thousand two hundred and seven, that's the exact number,' the King said, referring to his book. 'I couldn't send all the horses because two of them are still needed in the game. And I haven't sent my two Messengers, either. They've both gone to town. Could you just look along the road and tell me if you can see either of them.'

'I can see nobody on the road,' said Alice.

'I only wish I had such eyes,' the King remarked in a fretful tone. 'To be able to see Nobody! And at such a distance too! Why, it's as much as I can do to see real people, by this light.'

All this was lost on Alice, who was still looking intently down the road.

'I see somebody now!' she exclaimed at last, 'but he's coming very slowly and he's striking some very curious poses. Is that a dance he's doing?' (For the Messenger kept skipping up and down and then wriggling like an Eel as he came along.)

'Not at all,' said the King. 'He's an Anglo-Saxon Messenger and those are Anglo-Saxon attitudes. He only does them when he's happy. His name is Haigha.' (He pronounced it to rhyme with 'mayor'.)

'I love my love with an H,' Alice couldn't help but begin, 'because he is Happy. I hate him with an H because he is Hideous. I fed him with, with - Ham sandwiches and Hay. His name is Haigha, and he lives.......'

'He lives on the Hill,' the King remarked without the faintest idea that he was joining in the game, whilst Alice still struggled to think of a town beginning with H.'

'The other Messenger's called Hatta. I must have two, you know, to come and go.

'I beg your pardon? said Alice.

'It isn't respectable to beg,' admonished the King.

'I only meant that I didn't understand why you need to have one to come and one to go?' said Alice.

'Didn't I tell you?' the King repeated impatiently. 'I must have two. One to fetch and one to carry.'

At this moment the Messenger arrived. He was far too out of breath to say a word and only waved his hands about and made the most extraordinary faces at the poor King.

'This young lady loves you with an H,' the King announced abruptly.

Alice could feel her cheeks begin to flush red with embarrassment. She didn't love the Messenger with an 'H' or any other letter of the alphabet! Firstly she had never met him before in her entire life, secondly he was as mad as a March Hare and thirdly it seemed to Alice that he probably actually was a Hare.

Luckily the Messenger completely ignored the King's announcement and just made more strange gestures whilst rolling his eyes from side to side.

'You alarm me!' said the King 'I feel faint - Give me a ham sandwich!'

At which the Messenger, to Alice's great amusement, opened a bag that hung around his neck and handed a sandwich to the King who devoured it greedily.

'Another sandwich!' said the King.

'There's nothing but hay left now,' the Messenger said, peeping into the bag.

'Hay then,' the King faintly murmured. 'There's nothing like eating hay when you're faint,' he remarked to her as he munched.

'I should think throwing cold water over you might work better,' Alice suggested, 'or maybe some smelling salts.'

'I didn't say there was nothing better,' the King replied. 'I only said there was nothing like it. Now who did you pass on the road?' the King went on, holding out his hand to the Messenger for some more hay.

'Nobody,' said the Messenger.

'Quite right,' said the King. 'This young lady saw him too. So it's true what they say. Nobody walks slower than you.'

'I do my best,' the Messenger said in a sullen tone. 'I'm sure nobody walks much faster than I do!'

'He can't do that,' said the King, 'or else he'd have been here first. Now you've got your breath back you can tell us what happened in town.'

'I'll whisper it,' said the Messenger, putting his hands to his mouth in the shape of a trumpet and stooping so as to get close to the King's ear.

Alice felt a bit disappointed at this as she was hoping to be included in the news. However instead of whispering he simply shouted at the top of his voice, 'They're at it again!'

'Do you call that a whisper!' cried the poor King, jumping up and shaking himself. 'If you do such a thing again I'll have you cooked in a jug ! It went through and through my head like an earthquake!'

'Who are at it again?' asked Alice.

'Why the Lion and the Unicorn of course,' said the King.

'Fighting for the crown?'

'Yes, to be sure,' said the King, 'and the best of the joke is that it's my crown all the while! Let's run and see them.'

Montmartre,
Paris

Once again Mathers could feel the cold breath of time at his shoulder.

He had bathed, shaved his face and removed all of his rings and amulets.

For a moment he stood naked in front of the mirror and studied his reflection.

The face that stared back at him seemed older than he remembered, though the body was still lean and muscular. A testament to the daily bouts of harsh physical exercise he had forced himself to endure.

Mathers opened the door of the cupboard and removed a simple cotton gown from the rail where it was hanging . He placed his arms through the sleeves, slipped the gown over his head and let it drop.

There would be no crown or sword for tonight's ceremony, nothing but this thin sheet of cotton to separate him from the way he had first come into this world. For even a king must tread softly in the presence of his Maker.

Mathers carefully turned the brass handle of the outer door and entered the Temple. The room was lit only by the soft glow of candles and a shard of blue moonlight that filtered in through a gap at the top of the curtains.

In the centre of the floor there was a large gold painted pentagram within a circle, each of the star's five points touching the diameter, like arms outstretched to the universe. It was beautiful in its simplicity, but beauty must always contain at least one imperfection to elevate it from the superficial.

For what is music without silence, or day without night? Now he would have to embrace the darkest areas of his own nature and it was a journey from which there was no guarantee of return.

Mathers took a few minutes to clear his mind and control his breathing. He took deep slow inhalations, held down low in his diaphragm before being gently exhaled. No external thoughts could be allowed to intrude, his whole being would act as a lens, focused, powerful, precise.

With his breathing and heart rate slowed, he felt a burning energy surge around his body. He would use his mind to balance the power and submit it to his will. Only now was he ready to step into the circle. Sitting cross legged with his hands resting palms up on his knees, Mathers bowed his head forward and began to slowly chant:

'Comahon, Astarah, Macanah, Ratok, Astarah'

His voice broke the stillness of the Temple.

'Comahon, Astarah, Macanah, Ratok, Astarah'

The candles flickered as if in answer to his words.

'Comahon, Astarah, Macanah, Ratok, Astarah'

Mathers could feel the air around him becoming warmer and more humid as a gentle mist began to seep into the room.

'Comahon, Astarah, Macanah, Ratok, Astarah'

The temperature was still rising as the first beads of sweat ran down his neck to be absorbed in the cotton of his shirt. Rocking gently at first, Mathers' body soon began to sway as he lost himself in the rhythm of his chant, increasing in tempo, the last words catching up with the first until the whole became a single unified pulse.

'Comahon Astarah Macanah, Ratok Astarah
Comahon Astarah Macanah Ratok'

Forms were taking shape in the peripheries of the mist. Hideous and bestial, they were neither man nor beast but something altogether more ancient and monstrous.

Then came the sounds, barely audible at first, they rose and fell in time to his words. Wailing and tormented like nothing he had heard before, they echoed around the room in waves of a horrible intensity. Mathers sat suddenly still in the centre and bade his spirit lift from the Temple floor to rest above his earthly form.

Images rushed fast into his mind. The ruined palace of Solomon. Falcons soaring high above the Indus. Hashashins in the gardens at Alamut. A vortex in the house of the dead. White lakes of cloud above the dark horizon. Everything he had seen was returning in this moment. Unbound from the ties of reason and logic he would once again give himself over to fate.

The pressure in the air was heavy as the rain began to fall. A sudden bolt of lightning flashed outside, illuminating the evil

countenance of his audience below.

Thunder shook the window frames as Mathers surveyed the seething mass beneath him;

'*Behemot, Debac!*' he commanded and up through the roof into the rain-soaked sky he rose with the diabolic horde following close behind.

Alice repeated to herself as she ran the words of the old song:

The Lion and the Unicorn were fighting for the crown:
The Lion beat the Unicorn all around the town.
Some gave them white bread and some gave them brown:
Some gave them plum cake and drummed them out of town.

'And does - the one - that wins - get the crown?' she asked panting, as all the running was getting her a bit out of breath.

'Dear me, no,' said the King. 'What an idea!'

'Do you think that we could stop a minute?' asked Alice, 'just so I can get my breath back.'

'I'm afraid not,' the King replied. 'You see, we're not going fast enough. A minute goes by so fearfully quick. One might as well try to stop a Bandersnatch.'

She had no idea what he was talking about but neither did she have the energy for more questions, so now they trotted on in silence towards the fight.

Alice thought about the Jabberwock and her vow to fight the monster.

The idea had seemed a lot easier when she'd first said it but all this talk of fighting was bringing home the reality of her promise. To have any sort of chance she would need to find this Vorpal sword and quick!

Her thoughts were interrupted by the sight of a great crowd, in the middle of which were the Lion and the Unicorn. They were in such a cloud of dust, that at first Alice could not make out which was which but was soon able to distinguish the Unicorn by his horn. The crowd were happily cheering them on as the two went at each other ferociously. Alice felt a bit sickened to be a part of the whole spectacle but decided to remain quiet for now.

They placed themselves close to where Hatta, the other Messenger, was standing watching the fight. He had a cup of tea in one hand and a piece of bread and butter in the other.

'He's only just out of prison and he hadn't finished his tea when he was sent in,' Haigha whispered to Alice, 'and they only give them oyster-shells in there - so you see he's very hungry and thirsty. How are you, dear child?' he went on, putting his arm affectionately round Hatta's neck.

Hatta looked round and nodded and then got back to eating his bread and butter.

'Were you happy in prison?' said Haigha.

Hatta looked round once more and this time a tear or two rolled down his cheeks but he refused to say a word.

'Speak can't you?' Haigha cried impatiently. But Hatta only munched away and drank some more tea.

'Speak won't you?' cried the King. 'How are they getting on with the fight?'

Hatta made a desperate effort and swallowed a large piece of bread and butter. 'They're getting on very well,' he said in a choking voice. 'Each of them has only been down about eighty-seven times.'

'Then I suppose they'll soon bring the white bread and the brown?' Alice remarked.

'It's waiting for 'em now,' said Hatta. 'This is a bit of it I'm eating.'

There was a pause in the fight just then and the Lion and the Unicorn sat down panting while the King called out, 'Ten minutes allowed for refreshments!'

Haigha and Hatta were set to work at carrying around trays of white and brown bread. Alice took a piece to taste but it was quite stale and dry.

'I don't think they'll fight any more today,' the King said to Hatta.

'Go and order the drums to begin,' and Hatta went bounding away like a grasshopper.

For a minute or two Alice stood silently watching him. Suddenly she perked up. 'Look!' she cried, pointing excitedly. 'There's the Red Queen running across country! She came flying out of the wood. Those Queens can move really fast!'

'There's some enemy after her, no doubt.' said the King casually without even looking round. 'The whole wood's full of them.'

'But aren't you going to run and help her?' Alice asked, surprised at his lack of concern.

'No use, no use!' said the King. 'She runs so fearfully quick. You might as well try to catch a Bandersnatch! But I'll make a memorandum about her, if you like. She's a dear good creature,' he repeated softly to himself as he opened his notebook. 'Do you spell 'creature' with a double 'e'?'

At this moment the Unicorn came coolly sauntering by with his hands in his pockets. 'You know I had the best of it this time?' he said to the King, just glancing at him as he passed.

'A little - a little,' the King replied rather nervously. 'But you shouldn't have run him through with your horn, you know.'

'It didn't hurt him,' the Unicorn said carelessly, and he was about to walk on when his gaze happened to fall upon Alice. He turned round instantly and stood for some time looking at her with an air of the deepest disgust.

'What-is-this?' he said at last.

'This is a girl!' Haigha replied eagerly, in an attempt to impress. 'We only found it today. It's as large as life and twice as natural.'

'I always thought they were just fabulous monsters!' said the Unicorn. 'Is it alive?'

'It can talk,' said Haigha solemnly.

The Unicorn turned dreamily to Alice and said, 'Talk child.'

Alice could not help breaking into a smile as she began, 'Do you know I always thought Unicorns were fabulous monsters too! I never saw a real one before.'

'Well, now that we have seen each other,' said the Unicorn 'if you believe in me, I'll believe in you. Is that a bargain?'

'Yes, if you like.'

'Come fetch out the plum-cake, old man!' the Unicorn went on, turning from Alice to the King. 'None of your brown bread for me!'

'Certainly, certainly,' the King muttered beckoning to Haigha.

'Open the bag!' he whispered. 'Quick! Not that one, you fool - that's full of hay!'

Haigha took a large cake out of the bag and gave it to Alice to hold while he got out a dish and a carving knife. How all these things had fitted into the bag in the first place was difficult to know, as it wasn't really much more than a satchel. The scene reminded Alice of a conjuring trick she'd seen on television.

The Lion had joined them whilst this had been going on. He moved with a powerful grace, so relaxed it appeared almost lazy.

'What's this!' he asked in a deep booming voice that reverberated like the tolling of a large bell.

'Ah, what is it now?' the Unicorn cried out in amusement. 'You'll never guess! I couldn't.'

'It's a fabulous monster!' the Unicorn shouted out before Alice could reply.

'Then hand out the plum-cake, Monster,' the Lion said, lying down and resting his chin on his paws. 'Sit down both of you,' he commanded. 'Fair play with the cake, you know.'

The King looked very uncomfortable at being ordered around by this great beast but sat down between the Lion and the Unicorn as instructed.

'What a fight we might have now!' said the Unicorn, looking slyly up at the crown which nearly tumbled off the King's head, he was trembling so much.

'I should win easy,' said the Lion.

'I wouldn't be too sure of that,' said the Unicorn.

'Why, I'll beat you all around the town, you donkey!' the Lion replied angrily, half getting up as he spoke.

The King interrupted to try and stop the quarrel from getting out of hand but he was nervous so that his voice quivered as he spoke. 'All round the town?' he questioned. 'That's a good long way. Did you go by the old bridge or the marketplace? You get the best view from the old bridge.'

'I'm sure I don't know,' the Lion growled out as he lay down again. 'There was too much dust to see anything. What a time the monster is cutting up that cake!'

Alice had seated herself on the bank of a little brook, with the dish on her knees and was sawing away diligently with the knife. 'It's very frustrating!' she said in reply to the Lion. 'I've cut off several slices already but they just join back up again.'

'You don't know how to serve Looking-Glass cakes,' the Unicorn remarked. 'Hand it round first and cut it up afterwards.'

This sounded ridiculous, but Alice obediently got up and carried the dish round and sure enough, the cake divided itself into three pieces as she did so. 'Now cut it up,' said the Lion, as she returned to her place with the empty dish.

'I say, this isn't fair!' cried the Unicorn, as Alice sat with the knife in her hand, very much puzzled at how to begin. 'The Monster has given the Lion twice as much as me!'

'She's kept none for herself, anyhow,' said the Lion. 'Do you like plum-cake, Monster?'

But before Alice could answer, the drums began. Where the noise came from, she couldn't make out. The air seemed full of it and it rang through and through her head till she felt quite deafened. Alice sprang to her feet and in her alarm she jumped across the little brook. She looked back just in time to see the Lion and Unicorn rise from their seats, angry at having their feast interrupted, before she dropped to her knees and put her hands tightly over her ears in a vain attempt to shut out the overpowering din.

Loch Ness, Scottish Highlands

The moon had been rising since dusk and now sat high above the loch, shining like a spotlight on the ripples in the dark water below. Custom had it that these were perfect conditions for fishing, but there were few boats out on the loch tonight. Crowley stared up at the stars in the cloudless sky, gathered like spectators to his coming majesty. Before him lay a new frontier in human consciousness, a sacred awakening that would reveal to him the lost secrets of the infinite. He took one last look across the great expanse of water before turning up the bank towards Boleskine. He walked bare foot through the tall grass and along the trail of candles that led to the terrace and the open doors of his temple. He had seen this moment many times before, bathed in the warm sweat of opiate dreams or imagined by day in quiet meditation. But tonight was different, so still and serene, it was as if time itself had stopped in anticipation.

As Crowley took the final few steps towards the house he could see the blue reflected light criss-cross the hall leading up to the altar. The sign of Leucothea in Ascendence, for the White Goddess had risen to greet him.He turned to face the moon, dropped to his knees and began to softly chant:

'Doberah, Loharahos,Qeladim, Atsarah
Doberah, Loharahos,Qeladim, Atsarah.'

His voice grew in confidence and in volume with each repetition, until the words resembled more a challenge than a prayer

'Doberah, Loharahos,Qeladim, Atsarah
Doberah, Loharahos,Qeladim, Atsarah.'

Suddenly the sky darkened and a wind began to pick up off the water, scattering leaves from the trees as it whistled through their branches. Low clouds were moving fast across the horizon. Crowley rose from his knees, glanced up towards the heavens and bellowed:

'Doberah, Loharahos,Qeladim, Atsarah
Doberah, Loharahos,Qeladim, Atsarah.'

Again he shouted at the night before a burning fork of lightning struck the middle of the Loch. Then came thunder that roared and shook the ground beneath his feet and rain in sheets so dense his vision blurred as the water ran down his face like tears. Bracing his body to the wind he raged against the sky, daring God to smite him in his hour. But there was no answer, instead the wind eased, the rain stopped and an eerie silence settled over the loch. Not since Kanchenjunga in the shadow of Everest had he known such a strange and threatening emptiness. It was not just the weather that had changed, Crowley could feel a difference in himself too. It was as if all of his senses had been heightened by the storm. A wave of adrenalin rushed up through his body and flooded into his mind. He could make out beams of brilliant light flaring at the peripheries of his vision and a strange tortured music that was unlike anything he had ever heard before. Or could it be music at all? Whatever it was, it was getting louder, faster, closing in. Crowley turned to face Boleskine and there, up high above the roof were a horde of screaming demons framed against the burning sky. Crowley ran for the house, he had to turn the mirrors to the wall. Moving at an unnatural pace, he was across the terrace and into the corridor within seconds. But fear gripped his whole being as he heard their howls of murderous evil gaining on him from outside. He banged the doors shut behind him as he raced into the hall. The first mirror was to his left, and he was able to pull it roughly from the wall without breaking stride. The next was more difficult and he had to stop and grab the frame with both hands before dashing it to the ground. The glass cracked loudly on impact sending shards of broken silver scattering across the floor. Crowley ran on furiously down the corridor, tearing mirrors from the walls as he went.

He arrived at the end of the passage sweating and gasping for air. In front of him stood the Looking Glass calmly twinkling in the half-light, oblivious to the devastation of its kind. Crowley gazed into the glass, searching for any outward sign of the change he felt within. But all that reflected back at him was a trail of broken crystal leading out towards the night. He moved closer and blew gently on the mirror's surface. It misted over slightly where his image should have been but there was nothing of himself for he had become truly and utterly invisible.

Questions raced through his mind, 'What power could bestow such a gift and what now should he do with it?' He would not be held to the banal judgements of the weak. 'This is the law, do what thou wilt!' His thoughts were interrupted by the sound of a door creaking open on its hinges. From the corner of his eye he caught sight of something horrible moving in the glass.

Crowley spun on his heel to face the hallway.

The thing was creeping slowly up the corridor towards him, sniffing the air for a scent, touching the walls with its clawed misshapen hands, searching for a prey it could not see. Its powerful frame was covered in a thick matted fur and from the top of the brow protruded two short goatish horns. Just as the demons described by Abra Melin.

It stopped still, staring and listening for a movement or a breath. The Demon was gazing into the Looking Glass as if fascinated by its own reflection, 'like a grotesque Narcissus' thought Crowley to himself, 'then that must make me Nemesis'. Crowley surveyed the hallway. A long shard of broken glass lay almost within his reach.

Conscious not to make a sound, he carefully extended his left foot and pulled the shard gently towards him with his toes. It was close, tantalisingly close but not quite close enough. Keeping one eye fixed on the demon, he stretched out his leg once more and dragged the jagged splinter closer. Then suddenly, somehow, he slipped and his entire weight was brought down hard upon its sharp fractured edges. Crowley managed to stifle any cry of pain but he couldn't stop the flow of blood that was pulsing from his foot. Though his body remained invisible, his blood was spreading crimson across the polished wooden floor. The Demon smelt the blood before seeing it, flaring out its nostrils and breathing in deeply. Then it looked down the hall in the direction of Crowley's outstretched foot. There was no longer time to worry about noise, Crowley lurched forward and grabbed the shard. Sensing movement the Demon lifted its gaze from the bloodied floor and fixed its eyes quizzically on the glass in Crowley's hand. For a moment it stood thinking, before it came thundering down the corridor.

With his heart beating fast, Crowley waited until the thing was almost upon him, and tightening his grip on the glass dagger he plunged it with all his power deep into the monster's breast. Howling in pain the wounded creature lashed out its huge arms in an arc that found Crowley's back. Talons tore into his flesh and pulled him to its chest, crushing him close so that he could no longer breathe. Drifting in and out of consciousness he could see the beast begin to change. The fur was gone from its body and the face became more human and familiar. It began to resemble Mathers or was it Rosenkreuz or even Lazarus. Words rang loud in his head 'You would dare to battle me in the metaphysical, child?' Then it transformed again and became a King with a crown and white robes stained red with the blood that flowed from its chest.

Crowley struggled desperately to free himself as they fought, entwined like serpents in a final deadly embrace. He thrust himself up but stumbled backwards, taking the creature with him. Tripped, off balance and askew his adversary was sent crashing through the Looking Glass falling,

falling,

falling.

Chapter Eight

Alice lifted up her head in some confusion. There was no one to be seen. Her first thought was that she must have been dreaming about the Lion and the Unicorn. However, there was the great dish still lying at her feet, on which she had attempted to cut the plum-cake.

'So I wasn't dreaming, after all,' she told herself, 'unless...we're all part of the same dream. Well, if we are then I hope it's my dream, and not the White King's ! I don't want a bit part in someone else's dream. If only I could find a doctor to wake him, then I'd know for sure.'

These thoughts were suddenly interrupted by a coarse sounding voice that shouted out, 'Oi, you there! Check!'

'Who me?' answered Alice, nonplussed.

'Yes you, check!' came the gruff reply. 'I need to check you. What's your name and what are you doing here?'

'I'm sorry, my name's Alice and I'm trying to find a very particular type of sword,' said Alice politely.

The voice belonged to a Knight dressed in grimy, rust-red armour. He was brandishing an evil-looking club with sharp spikes on the end of it and he glared at Alice menacingly as he spoke.

100

The Knight put the club down and from inside his tunic produced a piece of tattered parchment which he proceeded to carefully unfold.

'Alice?' he repeated, scanning the parchment 'There's no Alice on here. No Alice, no Aleck, nothing. Your name's not on here,' said the Knight accusingly and he was right, her name was not on the parchment and nor was anyone else's, for the parchment was completely blank.

'I'm sorry', said Alice. 'I didn't know it had to be.'

'Oh really? You didn't know! And does that make it all right then? Did you really think you could just come strolling into this area without permission? I'm taking you to see my superior,' he growled, grabbing Alice by the arm and yanking her forcefully towards him.

Alice struggled desperately to free herself from his grip and in succeeding, fell head first into a rose bush. She instinctively put her hands out to break her fall and felt a pain sear along her left arm as it was dragged through a line of sharp thorns.

From this unwelcoming seat down amongst the roses Alice heard a new voice ring out.

'There appears to be a misunderstanding. This girl is my guest and does not need your permission to be here. Stand back from her now and we can all get on our way.'

The new voice belonged to a Knight dressed all in white. In contrast to the Red Knight, his armour was sparkling and immaculate. He stood facing the Red Knight and was staring directly into his eyes as he spoke, with a gaze that was steely and unflinching.

'She,..she's my prisoner and you've no right to interfere. It's the Queen's orders, n-no trespassers on Royal land,' the Red Knight stuttered out.

'Incorrect. She was your prisoner and I have every right. I carry a King's orders, not a Queen's and I advise you to leave this place now, whilst you find you are still able!'

With this he removed his left glove and threw it to the ground at the Red Knight's feet.

The Red Knight stared at the glove. Hesitating for a moment, he shook his head and mumbled something rude-sounding beneath his breath. He then heaved himself back up on to his horse and galloped away without ever looking back.

The White Knight walked calmly over to his glove and retrieved it before turning to Alice and offering a hand to help her up.

Still gingerly cradling her left arm, Alice grasped his right hand in her own right hand and let herself be gently hoisted to her feet.

'Please allow me to introduce myself,' said the Knight. 'I'm Sir John Lancaster but I'd be happy if you were to call me John.'

'Pleased to meet you, Sir John,' said Alice. 'My name's Alice.'

'Yes, I heard,' said the Knight with a smile, 'but my dear girl, you appear to have hurt your arm. Might I suggest you bathe it in the brook over there. You'll find the water clean if a little cold.'

The Knight removed his helmet and shook his hair out, then with both hands he tied his shaggy mane back behind his head. He was older than Alice had first thought, maybe as old as fifty, with a strong jaw, pronounced cheekbones and piercing blue eyes that nevertheless held some sort of kindness.

The pair of them walked the short distance to the brook together, the Knight's armour clanking as they went.

'So, Alice, what brings you to this side of the world? Do you have family here?' asked the Knight.

'Erm, no, it was more by accident really,' said Alice. 'I bought a looking glass, that was the beginning of it.'

The Knight thought for a moment before saying, 'Well, it's a happy sort of accident that brings someone like you as its result.'

Alice sat down on the bank, rolled up her left sleeve and slowly lowered her arm into the water. It felt cold but soothing on her torn skin. A group of small brightly coloured fishes flitted in and out of the reeds as Alice traced patterns lazily in the water above them with her fingertips.

'Who was that other man?' asked Alice, looking over at the Knight, 'the one who was trying to arrest me?'

'I know nothing of him. I've never seen him before today,' came the reply. 'The Red King's poor leadership has resulted in his Army taking heavy casualties and now the Red Queen will knight almost anyone that volunteers. Unfortunately his type have no real understanding of chivalry; it's an insult to our traditions.'

'Oh, I see,' said Alice. 'He got kind of rushed through. So you could say he was a late night. No wonder he was in a bad mood,' joked Alice.

'Quite right, and now he's been compelled to have an early night. Hopefully his temper will improve for it.' The Knight had walked back to his horse and began leading it towards where Alice lay.

'Does he have a name, your horse?'

'No, why? Should a horse have a name?' asked the Knight. 'I've had many other horses and none of them have had names.'

'Yes, he should. Is he fast?'

'He was once the fastest in all the Kingdom but like me, he's getting on now.'

'Well then, I think you should call him Full-Speed, like in full speed ahead!' said Alice.

'Full-Speed it is then,' answered the Knight, 'but I doubt he'll answer to his name as he doesn't know that he has one.'

'His metal anklets are quite serious looking. What are they for?' said Alice curiously.

'To guard against shark bites,' replied the Knight proudly. 'I made them myself.'

'Oh, I see... and are there a lot of sharks in the forest?' she added stifling a laugh that she attempted to disguise as a cough.

'Sometimes the sharks that live on the land are far worse than those in the water, that's something one learns with age,' said the Knight. 'By the way what's that dish for?' he asked Alice in return.

'It's meant for plum-cake,' said Alice.

'We'd better take it with us. It'll come in handy if we find any plum-cake,' said the Knight, handing her a saddlebag. 'Help me get it in this bag.'

Alice placed the dish carefully in the bag and handed it back to him. The Knight tied it on to his saddle next to where, rather strangely, there already hung a large bunch of carrots.

'I hope you don't mind me asking but why do you keep those carrots there?' Alice enquired.

'For Knight vision. But why not let me see you safely to the other side of the wood and we can talk some more as we go.'

So it was in this way that the two of them set off together, Alice walking happily next to the Knight and his horse as they passed slowly under the trees.

Sir John was a strange contradiction of a man, thought Alice. His job required him to be uncompromising and tough but at the same time he had an eccentric side that was really quite gentle.

'Alice, what's it like, the place where you are from?' he asked after they'd gone a short distance.

'Very different to here. It's not all woodland and brooks for a start. There are big buildings, people everywhere and motor cars and underground trains to get around on.'

'I don't think I'd like that, it sounds confusing,' said the Knight.

'You get used to it,' replied Alice.

'So my dear, what were you looking to do here? It's not a very nice place for a young girl to be on her own.'

'I was looking to find the Vorpal sword and I was hoping you might help me,' said Alice.

'And what would you want with any type of sword, let alone the Vorpal sword? It's not for everyone, the soldier's life. Doubtless you are brave and spirited but you're a young girl, you should be doing things that young girls do, not looking for swords and adventuring.'

'Somehow I have to do this, I thought you might help me, that's all,' said Alice dejectedly and so they walked on in silence for a while.

By now the sky had begun to darken and the wind was picking up, causing the branches of the trees to sway above them as it whirled through their leaves.

A rain announced itself with small spots that flecked in patterns across her dress before being absorbed into the cotton.

'Have you got your hair well fastened down?'

'Only with a band,' said Alice.

'Let's hope that's enough,' the Knight replied, 'the wind gets very strong as one gets close to the Tulgey Wood.'

'Is that where we're going?' asked Alice, her voice rising in alarm. She hadn't intended to go anywhere near the Tulgey Wood, at least not until she had found the Vorpal sword and had some time to practise with it.

'Yes, but there is no need to worry. I will protect you. I know this forest, likewise the people hereabouts. Nobody will dare threaten us.'

'But it isn't people that I'm worried about,' thought Alice.

'Can I ask you a question?' she said seriously, 'what kind of animal is the Jabberwock?'

'A good question and one that deserves an answer. For many years the Jabberwock was merely a legend of these dark woods. A formless terror whose name fuelled fear and superstition in equal measure. Then the King came and calmed it with strange words that soothed its savage nature. The beast became almost tame under his influence and loved the King like a dog loves its master. But now the King lies stricken and the Jabberwock blames us all. It rampages through our land like a plague.'

'Have you ever seen it?'

'Only from afar. Tell me, do they have the Ostrich bird where you are from?'

'Yes,' said Alice, 'in London Zoo.'

'And the serpent?'

'We have those too.'

'Well, the Jabberwock is something like both but fiercer than either.'

'Then you can see why I need the Vorpal sword,' said Alice.

107

'I doubt the Vorpal sword would make much difference. It would be best to stop thinking about such things. There is violence aplenty in this world without any need of a contribution from you. The course of my life is set but you have everything before you, there is...'

'There is no need to lecture me! You're not my dad, you know.' interrupted Alice.

The Knight frowned and paused a moment before answering, 'And what of your father. He shouldn't have allowed you to come here. Is he missing from your life?'

'I can't waste time talking about personal things which are actually none of your business,' said Alice angrily. 'Why don't you please just tell me where I can find the Vorpal sword instead!'

'Listen carefully to what I am about to tell you,' said the Knight seriously. '*The Book of Truths*' lies. There is no Vorpal sword. Did you think it would rise from a lake as in a fairy tale? For what is a sword if not a confused form of that power which it contains? Alice, the weapon you must use is words and the strongest word is Love. Love over all things will defeat the Jabberwock. You came here through a doorway that opens almost never. Why, Alice? By chance? A meaningless coincidence? The King is dying but he remembered that you would come and bade me wait to guide you. Many fear darkness but one small match in the blackest cave brings light and in this dark world you shine as brightly as a star.'

Alice was stunned into silence as her mind struggled to process what she'd just been told. Could you defeat a monster with words? What did he expect her to do? Calmly stroll up to it and say something nice and then they would all live happily ever after?

This seemed more like a fairy tale to Alice than any Vorpal

sword. And how had the King remembered her before she had even arrived?

'What exactly did the King tell you I should say to it?' asked Alice.

'He said that only words could defeat the Jabberwock and that you would know the words to say.'

The unfortunate fact was that she did not know. Maybe illness had made the King mistake her for someone else? Or this was all just part of some weird dream? But Alice didn't remember going to bed, so how could it be a dream?

She studied the Knight's lean features for any clue that he might be lying but could find none. Besides which, there was no reason for him to be lying. If he'd wanted to harm her he'd had plenty of opportunities to do so already. To fight the evil Jabberwock with just words? It didn't make any sense.

Maybe this was one of the impossible things the White Queen had told her she could believe in? Alice decided that she would have to try.

'Sir John, I will come with you to the Tulgey Wood but when we get there, can you promise me one thing?' said Alice, 'to lend me your sword? I think it would be best to have some sort of backup plan just in case the King has got things wrong.'

'Alice,' came the reply, 'I have never lent this sword to anyone and the King has never been wrong. But you may have the sword if that is what it will take to reassure you. Now let us make haste,' and with this the Knight kicked his left foot out of its stirrup and offered Alice a hand to help her up onto the saddle behind him. They trotted steadily away with Alice's arms locked around his waist for balance and her hair trailing out behind them as they headed on into the wind.

'Whatever happens now,' thought Alice, 'I'd better at least try and think of the right words to say. "I love you Jabberwock!" I could shout that at it, I suppose. But how is that going to work? Besides which, it's quite an embarrassing thing to have to shout.

Particularly if it's the last thing I ever get to say.'

It was dusk and the fading light had brought with it new, more sinister noises to replace the birdsong that filled the forest by day. She was glad the Knight was with her and that she would have a sword when they got to the Tulgey Wood, even if it wasn't going to be the Vorpal sword. The simple truth was that she didn't know any special way of taming a vicious animal or the words to do so. Alice decided she would need a more practical answer. She thought back to the final fencing lessons her father gave her. They were no longer just about technique but practical applications. 'Always choose your target early but do not let your opponent know it.' That was one tip. But the lesson he thought was the most important was not actually about fighting at all, it was about breathing.

'Alice, I hope you'll never have to use this but I am going to teach it to you anyway,' Dad had said. 'If you are ever in a situation where you are very scared, your natural reactions will take over. You'll feel a lot of adrenalin suddenly in your body which will make your legs start to feel a bit shaky. It's at this point that you have to decide whether running or fighting is the best option. If it's to run, then just run as fast as you can, but if you can't run and have to fight, then concentrate on your breathing. You must breathe low in your stomach like a singer, not high up in your throat like you normally would. And always in through your nose, not your mouth.'

Alice used to find this quite nice and relaxing standing with her eyes closed, opposite Dad in the warm sports hall. It wasn't so relaxing now as she practised up on the back of a horse, at the back of beyond with a monster in waiting.

The wind had been getting stronger all along their journey and now she couldn't make out what Sir John was saying above its roar, but he was gesturing towards a small wooden gate that stood at the end of the track they'd been riding down.

Full-speed did not like this place any more than Alice. He began to whinny and snort, throwing his head to one side as Sir John pulled back on the reins to slow him to a stop.

Sir John lowered himself down from the saddle and held the horse still whilst speaking reassuringly to it so that Alice could get herself safely to the ground.

He then tethered him to a nearby post and began unpacking things from one of the saddlebags. He addressed Alice without looking at her whilst he busied himself with this.

'That gate marks the entrance to the Tulgey Wood. My instructions were only to guide you to this point but I have decided to stay. We shall make camp here tonight as, no matter what the King has said of the future, it would not be right to leave you here alone.'

'Thank you.' said Alice unable to conceal the relief in her voice, 'It means a lot. I'm going to take a quick look around and then I could help you unpack.'

'Whilst you do that, see if you can find some kindling for a fire. Fallen branches, dry twigs, that sort of thing.'

Alice walked cautiously over toward the gate scanning her path for kindling but also for imagined dangers she half expected to jump out from the darkness at her.

The moon had risen now and under its soft glow she was able to pick out some of the details of her surroundings. Next to the gate was a ditch and at the bottom of this were dotted shallow pools of stagnant water. The ditch ran the length of the track like a border and on the other side of it, the landscape began to change. There were no longer any large oaks or cedars here, only a thinner variety of tree that Alice hadn't ever seen before. These new trees were not just thin, they were mean looking, their branches sparse and broken as if neglected by nature herself. There was something both hopeless and threatening about this place and Alice was scared of it. She turned and hurried back picking up any fallen twigs that she saw on her way. On arriving, she found Sir John had laid two blankets on the ground next to a pile of branches around which he was now carefully arranging a circle of stones.

'Ah, there you are, my dear.' said Sir John. 'This is the best shape for a fire, we'll put those twigs of yours down in the middle with some pine cones and it should hopefully last the night.'

He took a match from a silver case and struck it on the rough surface of one of the stones. The fire crackled as it caught and Alice sat down out of the wind to warm her hands. Strangely, here under the moonlight, watching sparks from the fire dance up into the cold night air she felt free for the first time in years. Her exams didn't matter any more, even school didn't matter.

There was nothing but the Jabberwock and maybe nothing after.

'This sword is yours now Alice, for when you vanquish the Jabberwock I will have no further need of it.'

She looked up to see Sir John holding the sword by its scabbard as he passed it, handle first, towards her. Alice took the sword from him. It was heavy, much heavier than anything she had ever fenced with and more elaborately designed too. The handle had a golden cross-guard that met the blade at its hilt and its other end was a round pommel decorated with a single ruby.

'I'm really grateful,' said Alice 'but I only want to borrow it for a bit and besides you are a Knight, what if someone challenges you to a duel or something?'

'A duel?' said Sir John smiling. 'Well, in that case it may be that you'll have to come and defend my honour.'

'Of course I will' said Alice 'but anyway, I suppose it would be better to just try and get on with people.'

Suddenly an owl flew out from the branches above them, and shortly after this it started: a faint, distant howling barely discernable above the wind.

'Did you hear that?' whispered Sir John. 'Keep down whilst I go to the horse to fetch my bow.'

He moved quickly, keeping his body low as he covered the ground. The noise, no longer faint, had distorted into a kind of high pitched screech that echoed its menace across the sky. Alice didn't need to be told the source of this horrible sound. An evil call that was falling over itself in ambition to reach her.

She could feel the adrenalin surge through her body in waves. Everything outside seemed to slow down but inside things were speeding. 'Too fast,' thought Alice, 'got to breathe.' She took long deep breaths, breathing in through her nose and far down into her stomach. 'Time to decide. Do I fight or run? Running would be good,' thought Alice, 'away from this place. Back to the living room, back through the mirror and home safe.'

But standing up into the wind, it felt as if she were being pulled by some great unseen force, drawing her irresistibly. Then Sir John was at her side.

'Do you remember the words yet?' he asked urgently.

'No, not yet.' Alice replied.

'I can distract it with arrows from the left flank, but try to think, Alice, you must remember, everything here depends on you!'

The sword felt heavy, her feet felt heavy but on she trudged.

Now she was at the gate. Though they had warned her of this thing, no-one had prepared her for its smell. A sulphurous filth carried on the wind that even the rain could not dampen down.

Once past the gate she stopped.

Ahead of her was the wood and there in the distance was the Jabberwock.

Alice was frozen in a mixture of horror and fascination. The creature had a long reptilian tail and a neck that snaked ever up-wards to a huge fish-like head. The head resembled something that might live in the lowest depths of the darkest ocean whilst the rest of it looked more suited to the land.

Short-winged like some great flightless bird but with talons fit to tear metal, the Jabberwock was searching for something. Scouring the terrain from left to right before it craned its long neck up above the trees and focused its stare directly on Alice. For a moment, it was still. For a moment only, it seemed undecided then a flicker of recognition flashed across its fiery eyes and it spat.

A stream of hissing sputum arced high up into the air and scorched the earth where it landed.

Now the Jabberwock came pounding towards her, howling and screaming as it ran. Alice tightened her grip on the sword. There would only be the time for one shot at this and afterwards, only words.

Alice tried desperately to lift the sword to head height, her every sinew straining from the effort. She managed to get it just behind her right shoulder. The Jabberwock was close, close enough that she could see the slobber spill from its snarling mouth. Alice could feel her legs begin to go weak as a nauseous fear rose in the pit of her stomach.

Her wrists were shaking so much she couldn't hold the sword any longer and let it drop. Though her heart was racing, the rest of her stood frozen. The beast was nearly upon her when the first arrow struck with a thunk! The Jabberwock gave out a howl of pain as the arrow pierced its scaly flesh and reeled its great head round.

'Here! I'm over here, you ugly brute!' Sir John called out, while quickly threading another arrow into his bow. He was standing on some raised scrubland about twenty metres along the ditch from Alice. The bow flexed as he drew the string back and took aim once again.

'Come on, you monster. It's me you want now!'

The second arrow hit the Jabberwock just above its hooded eye as it launched itself with bewildering speed in the direction of its torment.

Colours and shapes and action blurred together before Alice

saw Sir John in the clamp of the beast's powerful jaws which shook him from side to side as if he were nothing more than a rag doll. Then, as though bored, suddenly it stopped, and threw him disdainfully into the air. For a while his body flew upward until his full weight met the trees with a sickening crack and he dropped to the ground where he lay limp and unmoving.

Alice couldn't believe what she'd just seen.

A flash of lightning burnt through the night, illuminating this stark horror like a strobe and out of it came death thundering towards her. Could she bring herself to say it now? After this!

'I love you Jabberwock,' Alice whispered under her breath but to no avail. Still the beast came on. It seemed so stupid that this was how her life would end. She thought again about what Sir John had said. 'What is a sword if not a confused form of the power it contains?' A sword made of letters, a word. A sword is a word and words can make a sword. 'It's an anagram!'

She tried to shout, but what came out was:

'*D ebam*
R echem
E rera
A rere
M abed'

These strange single words, fired out in quick succession booming in velocity like gunfire. With its momentum halted, the creature lurched and stumbled as if in a drunken dance to each syllable as it careered towards her. The powerful legs buckled from under it and its neck sagged from the weight of the great head that was flailing and snapping at the air as it toppled over and landed at Alice's feet with a crash. The Jabberwock now prone, stared up into Alice's eyes with an expression both fearful and venomous. Then inexplicably, the creature started to shrink. First its wings disappeared up into its haunches then the torso lengthened out and the head flattened.

As Alice looked down at the shrinking Jabberwock, it seemed like a terrible weight had been lifted from it and in place of hatred in its eyes there was gratitude. No longer a monster, it resembled nothing more than a harmless grass snake.

Alice placed her right foot directly over its head. Now that she had all the power, Alice could extinguish this creature's life with one stamp, (and for a split second she considered it.) 'But that would make me the monster,' thought Alice, 'and what about Sir John? I have to help Sir John!' Alice stepped over the small snake at her feet and began to sprint.

'Make him be all right,' Alice told herself as she ran. But what she'd seen in the lightning didn't look all right. It did not look all right at all.

As she got closer, Alice began to slow her pace.

At first glance Sir John's body looked normal as it rested motionless beneath the ragged trees. Some freshly broken branches were scattered around and Alice hoped these might have been enough to cushion his fall, but as she got nearer still, her heart sank. His left leg was rotated at an unnatural angle and raw bone jutted from the shin below. Though she found it difficult to look, she knelt beside him and gently squeezed his hand in her own.

She felt him grip her hand tightly in return and then his eyes blinked open. Despite wincing, he managed to smile through the pain as he spoke.

'I knew you could do it.'

'I didn't do it.' said Alice, looking deeply into his eyes. 'We did it. Now I need you to save your energy while I work out how to get you moved from here.'

'It's getting so dark and cold, I fear there's no use in that,' said Sir John. ' You've only a few yards to go, down the hill and over the brook, and then you'll be a Queen but you'll stay and see me off first? I shan't be too long. You'll wait and wave your handkerchief when you get to that turn in the road? I think it'll encourage me, you see.'

'Of course I'll wait,' said Alice, her voice breaking as she forced back tears.

'I'm very proud of you, my girl. Don't cry, it's just my time, that is all. Alice, I think you will be the best Queen there ever was.' With that he closed his eyes and Alice felt his grip loosen on her fingers. She stayed there with him holding his hand even after his arm had dropped and his breath had slowed to nothing. Then she fumbled for the handkerchief in the pocket of her skirt and stood and waved it over him before turning to walk downhill towards the brook.

Alice felt completely numb. She'd somehow used words that she'd never learnt, to fight a monster that had killed the only friend she had made in this horrible place. None of it made any sense and none of it was nice at all.

The Looking Glass was magic or haunted or both, that much was clear, but why had she been chosen to find it?

Alice did not know how or even if she could get a proper burial for Sir John, but if she became Queen then maybe she could order it to be done. Whilst thinking all this over, she was soon at the edge of the brook.

The distance to the bank on the other side wasn't great but the water looked deep and uninviting. Alice took a few steps back and ran at the gap, easily clearing the brook and landing on the opposite side on grass as soft as moss.

It felt comforting to lie down in the soft grass. 'Maybe there's something wrong with me?' thought Alice. 'It can't be normal to just to want to lie down here like this after everything that's happened. I feel as if I'm becoming as mad as everything else here.' But she was so tired that she couldn't help but close her eyes and drift off.

*   *   *

Alice awoke to a strange sensation of tightness around her temples. Her head seemed somehow to have got heavier while she had been asleep, it was even an effort to lift it off the grass. She sat up and rubbed the sleep from her eyes before putting her hands up to find something cold and heavy, fitted tight on top of her head.

'That's bizarre! How can it have got there without my know-ing?' said Alice to herself as she lifted it off and set it down on her lap. For resting there on her knees, twinkling in the early morning sunlight, was a real golden crown.

'It's not good form for you to be lolling about on the grass like that! Queens have to be dignified,' said Alice reprimanding her-self in a clipped upper-class accent, so she got up and practised walking about with the crown balanced precariously on the top of her head.

It took some time, but eventually she was able to walk about without worrying that at any moment her new headgear might come tumbling off. Then Alice adjusted the crown to a slightly more casual angle and practised that too. Once she was satisfied with her performance she sat back down. Alice was deep in her own thoughts when she became aware of a presence close by. She looked around and saw that both the Red Queen and White Queen were sitting one on either side of her and not more than an arm's length away.

'I need to know if I'll be treated like a proper Queen now I've got this crown on my head,' thought Alice, so she decided to speak up.

'Can one of you tell me if I am now really a Queen?'

'Speak when you're spoken to!' the Red Queen sharply interrupted her.

'But if I obeyed that rule and only spoke once I was spoken to, and other people also obeyed the rule so that they were waiting to be spoken to, then nobody would ever say anything,' replied Alice.

'Ridiculous!' cried the Queen. 'Why, don't you see, child -' here she broke off with a frown and, after thinking for a minute, suddenly changed the subject. 'What do you mean by "If you really are a Queen?" What right have you to call yourself so? You can't be a Queen, you know, until you've passed the proper examination. And the sooner we begin it the better.'

'I only said if,' replied Alice in her own defence.

The two Queens looked at each other, and the Red Queen remarked with a shudder, 'She says she only said if.'

'But she said a great deal more than that!' the White Queen moaned, 'ever so much more.'

'So you did, you know,' the Red Queen admonished Alice. 'Always speak the truth - think before you speak - and write it down afterwards.'

'I didn't mean-' Alice began but the Red Queen interrupted her impatiently. 'That's just what I complain of! You should have meant! What do you suppose is the use of a girl without any meaning? Even a joke should have some meaning- and a girl is more important than a joke, I hope. You couldn't deny that even if you tried with both hands.'

'I don't deny things with my hands,' objected Alice.

'Nobody said you did,' said the Red Queen. 'I said you couldn't if you tried.'

'She's in that state of mind,' said the White Queen 'that she wants to deny something - only she doesn't know what to deny!'

'A nasty vicious temper,' remarked the Red Queen and then there was an uncomfortable silence for a minute or two.

After a while the Red Queen broke the tension by saying to the White Queen, 'I invite you to Alice's dinner party this afternoon.'

The White Queen smiled feebly and said 'And I invite you.'

'I didn't know I was having a party,' said Alice 'but if I am then I think it ought to be up to me to invite the guests.'

'We gave you the opportunity,' the Red Queen remarked, 'but I daresay you've not had many lessons in manners yet?'

'Manners are not taught in lessons,' said Alice. 'Lessons teach you sums and history and that sort of thing.'

'Can you do addition?' asked the White Queen. 'What's one and one and one and one and one and one and one and one and one and one and one and one and one?'

'I don't know,' said Alice. 'I lost count.'

'She can't do addition,' declared the Red Queen. 'Can you do subtraction? Take nine from eight and eight from that, and what do you have?'

'I'm not sure,' said Alice.

'Eight from that leaves ta, which is not a polite way to thank someone who's only trying to teach you manners.'

'She can't do subtraction,' declared the Red Queen. 'Can you do division? Divide a loaf by a knife - what's the answer to that?'

'I suppose,' Alice began but the Red Queen answered for her. 'Bread and butter, of course. Try another subtraction sum. Take a bone from a dog and what remains?'

Alice decided to consider this carefully before replying. 'The bone wouldn't remain because I would have taken it and so the dog wouldn't remain; it would probably come to bite me which means I don't think I'd remain there either.'

'Then you think nothing would remain?' said the Red Queen.

'Yes, I think that's the answer,' replied Alice.

'Wrong, as usual,' said the Red Queen, 'the dog's temper would remain.'

'But I don't really see how-'

'Why, look here!' the Red Queen cried impatiently, 'the dog would lose its temper, wouldn't it?'

'It probably would,' said Alice.

'Then if the dog went away, its temper would remain!' the Queen exclaimed.

'They might go different ways,' said Alice in a tone of irritation, before reminding herself not to get angry as in fact the whole conversation was completely ridiculous.

'She can't do sums a bit!' both Queens shouted out in unison.

'Well, can you do sums?' asked Alice to the White Queen. 'you've been a bit quiet up till now.'

The Queen gasped and shut her eyes. 'I can do addition,' she said 'if you give me time - but I can't do subtraction under any circumstances!'

Here the Red Queen started up once more. 'Can you answer

useful questions?'

'Sometimes,' replied Alice.

'Well then, how is bread made?' asked the Red Queen.

'First, you take some flour,' said Alice patiently.

'Where do you pick the flower? In a garden or in the hedges?' asked the Red Queen.

'It isn't that type of flower,' said Alice wearily, 'it's not picked, it's ground.'

'How many acres of ground?' said the White Queen. 'You mustn't leave out the detail.'

'Fan her head!' instructed the Red Queen. 'She'll be feverish after so much thinking.' So they both set to work fanning her head with bunches of leaves which Alice found quite annoying as she was not feverish at all and the leaves kept hitting her on the nose.

'She's all right now,' said the Red Queen. 'Do you know the cause of lightning?'

'The cause of lightning is the thunder...actually no,' she corrected herself, 'I think it's the other way round.'

'It's too late to correct it,' said the Red Queen, 'when you've once said a thing, that fixes it and you must take the consequences.'

The White Queen gave a deep sigh, and laid her head upon Alice's shoulder.

'I feel so sleepy,' she said yawning.

'She's tired, poor thing!' said the Red Queen. 'Smooth her hair - lend her your nightcap - and sing her a soothing lullaby.'

'I don't own a nightcap and I don't know any soothing lullabies,' explained Alice.

'I must do it myself then,' said the Red Queen, and she sang:

'Hush a by lady in Alice's lap!
Till the feast's ready, we've time for a nap:
When the feast's over, we'll go to the ball-
Red Queen and White Queen and Alice, and all!'

'And now you know the words,' she added as she put her head down on Alice's other shoulder, 'just sing it through to me. I'm quite sleepy too.'

In another moment both Queens were fast asleep and snoring loudly.

'Blimey, what am I supposed to do?' exclaimed Alice, looking about in some confusion as first one head then the other rolled down from her shoulder, and lay like a heavy boulder in her lap. 'I don't think this could have ever happened before, that anyone had to take care of two Queens asleep at once. Do wake up, you great lumps!' exclaimed Alice, but there was no answer but a gentle snoring.

The snoring got louder every minute it until it began to sound almost musical, and Alice felt sure she could pick out a distinct though basic melody. She was listening for this so intently that when the two big heads vanished from her lap she hardly noticed they had gone.

Alice found herself standing before an arched doorway, over which the words QUEEN ALICE were carved in large letters, and on each side of it there was a bell handle; one was marked 'Visitor's bell' and the other 'Servant's bell'.

'I'll wait until that awful song is over,' thought Alice, 'and then I'll ring the bell– but which one should I ring? I'm not a visitor and I'm definitely not a servant. There ought to be one marked Queen.'

Just then the door opened a little way, and a creature with a long beak put its head out for a moment and said, 'No admittance till the week after next!' And shut the door again with a bang.

'Do you know who I am!' shouted Alice through the letterbox. 'I'm Queen Alice, open the door immediately. Come and look, there's my name above it!' Alice knocked and rang in vain for a long time until at last a very old Frog who was sitting under a tree got up and hobbled slowly towards her; he was dressed all in velvet and had enormous boots on his feet.

'What is it now?' the Frog asked in a deep hoarse whisper.

Alice turned around angrily 'Where's the person whose job it is to answer the door?' she began.

'Which door?' said the Frog.

Alice almost stamped in irritation at the inanity of the question and the slow drawl in which it was asked. 'This door, of course!'

The Frog looked at the door with his large dull eyes for a minute; then he went nearer and rubbed it with his thumb, as if he were seeing if the paint would come off, and then he looked at Alice.

'To answer the door?' he said. 'Why, what's it been asking?' He said this in a voice so hoarse that Alice could hardly make out what he was saying.

'I don't know what you mean,' said Alice, tired of the incessant nonsense.

'I speaks English, doesn't I?' the Frog went on, 'or are you deaf? What did it ask you?'

'Nothing!' said Alice impatiently. 'I've just been knocking at it!'

'Shouldn't do that - shouldn't do that,' muttered the Frog.

'Vexes it you know.' Then he went up and gave the door a kick with one of his great feet. ' You let it alone,' he panted out as he hobbled back to his tree 'and it'll let you alone, you know.'

At this moment the door was flung open, and a shrill voice was heard singing:

'To the Looking-Glass world it was Alice that said
I've a sceptre in hand, I've a crown on my head;
Let the Looking-Glass creatures wherever they be
Come dine with the Red Queen, the White Queen and me!'

And hundreds of voices joined in the chorus:

> 'Then fill up the glasses as quick as you can,
> And sprinkle the table with buttons and bran,
> Put cats in the coffee and mice in the tea -
> And welcome Queen Alice with thirty times three.'

There followed a confused noise of cheering, and Alice thought to herself 'Thirty times three makes ninety. I wonder if anyone's counting?'

For a minute there was silence again and then the same shrill voice sang another verse:

> 'O Looking-Glass creatures', quoth Alice draw near!
> 'Tis an honour to see me, a favour, you hear?
> 'Tis a privilege high to have dinner and tea
> Along with the Red Queen, the White Queen and me!'

Then came the chorus again:

> 'Then fill up the glasses with treacle and ink,
> Or anything else that is pleasant to drink;
> Mix sand with the cider and wool with the wine-
> And welcome Queen Alice with ninety times nine!'

'Ninety times nine?' Alice repeated to herself. 'What a bore, that welcome is going to take forever. I'd better go in straight away,' and so in she went.

There was a hushed silence the moment she appeared and instead of people enjoying themselves, they only seemed interested in looking at her and what she was wearing.

Alice glanced nervously along the table as she walked up the large hall, and noticed that there were about fifty guests in all kinds of costumes. Some were animals, some birds and there were even a few flowers amongst them. Although they all seemed to know one another, Alice didn't know any of them and there were murmurs as she passed by.

'I'm glad they've come without me having to ask them,' thought Alice ' I wouldn't have known all these people to invite.'

There were three chairs at the head of the table; the Red and White Queens had taken two of them, but the middle one was empty. Alice sat down, rather uncomfortable at the silence and hoped that someone would speak.

At last the Red Queen began. 'You've missed the soup and fish,' she said. 'Put on the joint!' And a waiter set a leg of mutton before Alice, who looked at it rather anxiously, as she had never had to carve one before.

'You look a little shy; let me introduce you to that leg of mutton,' said the Red Queen.

'Alice - Mutton; Mutton - Alice.'

The leg of mutton got up in the dish and made a little bow to Alice, and she returned the bow not knowing what to do next.

'Am I supposed to give you a slice?' she said, taking up the knife and fork and looking from one Queen to the other.

'Certainly not,' the Red Queen said very decidedly. 'It isn't etiquette to cut anyone you've been introduced to. Remove the joint!'

And to Alice's great relief the waiters carried it off and brought a large plum pudding in its place.

'I'd better not be introduced to the pudding or nobody'll get any dinner at all. May I give you some?' asked Alice.

But the Red Queen looked sulky and growled, 'Pudding - Alice; Alice - Pudding. Remove the pudding!'

And the waiters took it away before Alice could return its bow.

However, she was a Queen now and didn't see why the Red Queen should be the only one to give orders, so, as an experiment, she called out, 'Waiter! Bring back the pudding!' and it appeared again in a moment. She immediately cut a slice and gave it to the Red Queen.

'What impertinence!' said the pudding. 'I wonder how you'd like it, if I were to cut a slice out of you, you creature!' Its voice was thick and suety as though it were speaking through a winter scarf.

'I beg your pudding,..I mean pardon,' said Alice, flustered by the realisation of what she had just done.

'Say something else,' said the Red Queen. 'It's ridiculous to leave all the conversation to the pudding!'

Alice had no idea what to say so she just said the first thing that came into her head which was, 'Do you know, I've had such a lot of poetry recited to me today…'

The moment she started speaking the room grew silent so that you could hear a pin drop and all eyes fixed upon her but she somehow carried on…'and I think every poem mentioned fishes….do you know why, erm….everyone's so fond of fishes around here?'

'Well, that was just about the stupidest thing I could have said!' thought Alice to herself.

But somehow the Red Queen seemed interested. 'As to fishes,' she said, very slowly and solemnly putting her mouth close to Alice's ear 'Her White Majesty knows a lovely riddle - all in poetry - all about fishes. Should she repeat it?'

'Her Red Majesty's very kind to mention it,' said the White Queen and so she began:

> 'First the fish must be caught.'
> That is easy: a baby, I think, could have caught it.
> 'Next the fish must be bought.'
> That is easy: a penny I think would have bought it.
>
> 'Now cook me the fish.'
> That is easy, and will take more than a minute.
> 'Let it lie in a dish!'
> That is easy, because it already is in it.
>
> 'Bring it here, let me sup!'
> It is easy to set such a dish on the table.
> 'Take the dish-cover up!'
> Ah, that is so hard that I fear I'm unable!
>
> For it holds it like glue-
> Holds the lid to the dish, while it lies in the middle:
> Which is easiest to do,
> Un-dish-cover the fish, or dishcover the riddle?'

'Take a minute to think about it, and then guess,' said the Red Queen. 'Meanwhile we'll drink to your health – to Queen

Alice, slayer of the Jabberwock!' she screamed at the top of her voice and all of the guests immediately began drinking to her. However, they went about this in a most revolting way. Some put their glasses on their heads and drank all that dribbled down their faces whilst others upset the decanters and drank the wine greedily as it ran off the edges of the table. Three of them even scrambled into the roasting dish and began to lap up the gravy with their tongues.

'So these are my very important guests?' thought Alice to herself, 'they don't have any manners at all.'

'You ought to return thanks with a short speech,' said the Red Queen, frowning at Alice as she spoke.

'We must support you, you know,' the White Queen whispered as Alice reluctantly got up to speak.

'I think I'll be all right on my own, thanks.' Alice whispered back.

'That wouldn't be the done thing at all,' said the Red Queen firmly.

So Alice decided to try and submit to it with good grace. This proved quite difficult as their idea of support seemed to be to push her from opposite directions until she was nearly lifted off her feet.

'I rise to return thanks -' began Alice, and she really did rise as she spoke, several inches in fact, but she somehow got hold of the edge of the table, and managed to pull herself down again.

'Calm down!' screamed the White Queen, seizing Alice's hair with both hands, 'or something's going to happen!'

And then all sorts of things did start to happen.

First the candles shot up to the ceiling, looking something like a bed of rushes with an explosion of fireworks at the top.

132

Then the bottles each took a pair of plates, which they fitted on as wings and with forks for legs went whizzing wildly about the room. As the chaos started to unfold, Alice heard a raucous laugh at her side and turned to see what the White Queen was finding so funny about the alarming situation.

But instead of the White Queen, it was the leg of mutton sitting in her chair.

'Here I am!' cried a voice from the soup-tureen and Alice turned again just in time to see the Queen's broad good-natured face grinning nervously at her before it disappeared into the soup with a plop. There was no time to be lost. Already several of the guests were lying down drunk in the dishes and the soup ladle was walking up towards Alice's chair, gesturing angrily for her to get out of the way.

'I can't stand this any longer!' she cried, as she jumped up and seized the tablecloth with both hands: one good pull, and plates, dishes, guests, and candles came crashing down together in a heap on the floor.

'And as for you,' she said, turning angrily to the Red Queen, but all she saw was a flash of the Red Queen's shawl heading swiftly out the door.

Alice decided to go after her and ran down the hall and out into the open air letting the door bang shut behind her.

She was running fast, so fast that her feet hardly touched the ground before they were up again for another step. 'So this is how they do it,' thought Alice to herself. 'It's fun.'

As she sped back through the landscape of her journey, everything had changed. The sky was blue and cloudless and under it even the Tulgey Wood had lost some of its menace. A warm afternoon sun bathed the trees in light and the fields, no longer desolate, were swathed in vibrant green, with patches of colour where daffodils and crocuses had broken through the soil.

Alice looked for Sir John beneath the tree where she last left him, but his body had vanished and in its place there sat a single white dove. She stood quietly watching the bird for a while before starting off again. Alice could now travel at such speeds that within moments she was at the top of the hill with the house clearly visible in the near distance. In fact, she was going so fast that it was as much as she could do to slow down and avoid crashing into the garden gate. Alice straightened her tattered dress and walked up the path to the house with as much dignity as she could muster.

It was a relief to find that the door was still unlocked and Alice let herself in quietly. Opposite her stood the old wooden staircase and she walked over and tentatively placed her foot on the bottom step. The first pressure of her foot on the stair started the familiar rumbling motion and soon she was at the top.

Everything was in the same place. There was the large fireplace with coals burning. The furniture was heavy and brown and the clock on the wall counted out time with a gentle tick.

Although in the ashtray smoke still curled from a smouldering cigarette, the cigarette itself had not burnt down any further at all.

Over by the window there was the mahogany writing desk with its neatly stacked note paper. Alice walked up to it and examined the writing once again. There it was, the sole unanswered question: 'Will she return?'

How long she had been in this distorted world was impossible to tell but the mirror glass was beginning to brighten and she knew it would soon be time for her to leave. Alice stared at the words on the page intently before picking up the pen and inscribing, 'NEVAR' beneath them in large purple letters.

Alice couldn't say that she had enjoyed this journey.

There was an expression she'd heard used that was supposed to be profound. It was probably invented by someone famous.

'What doesn't kill you makes you stronger.'

'What doesn't kill me has failed to kill me and that's all I really know about it,' thought Alice to herself.

Her body was tired from everything it had been put through and her mind even more so. It felt as if every rule that she'd been taught to respect had been challenged and undermined. To be a Queen, that was something you were supposed to want, wasn't it? All she wanted right now was to be at home and do normal things again.

Alice approached the Looking Glass. Though the person staring back at her was clearly still herself, Alice felt she had changed and that somehow things could never be quite the same again. She dropped her head and raised an eyebrow.

'Really?' Alice asked herself in a low voice that belied her years. 'Yes, really,' she answered in reply.

Alice took the chair from behind the desk and used it to climb up onto the edge of the mantelpiece. Stepping confidently into her own reflection, the glass gave way like a giant wisp of candyfloss.

Once in this misty corridor Alice could vaguely make out the sound of a bell chiming as she edged towards the light. The sound did not diminish but was actually becoming louder and more persistent. No longer chiming, the bell was now an intrusive ringing in her ears that carried through a fog of confused thoughts. Alice yawned and rubbed her eyes. She was lying on the living room sofa, her head half buried into one of the cushions with the telephone still loudly ringing out. Whoever was on the other end of it was obviously quite stubborn, or else? Alice jumped up and ran for the phone but just as she managed to juggle the receiver into her hands, the ringing abruptly stopped. As Alice replaced the receiver she began to try and work things through in her mind.

'So it was all just a dream,' thought Alice, 'but what about the Looking Glass? Did I really dream that as well?'

She glanced back over her shoulder and there it was, still leaning against the wall, an imposing presence towering above a small sea of torn brown wrapping paper. Just then the telephone started ringing again. Alice reached down easily with her left hand and answered it.

'Hello?'

'Hello, is that Miss Liddell?'

The man's voice sounded confident and enthusiastic and not someone that Alice recognised from her Mum's circle of friends.

'Yes, I'm Alice Liddell. Is it me you wanted to talk to or my Mum?'

'Actually it's you that I want to speak to. Now Alice, I have some very good news for you. I have been trying to track down some property. I was given your number by Graham at the Peacehaven store and he says you purchased a mirror today which is the reason for my call. Listen, I've sent you an email as well but I'm glad I've caught you at home so that I can explain it personally. I work for a man, a very wealthy man – a collector of rare and beautiful things.'

'It was a Looking Glass I bought today,' Alice interrupted.

'Looking Glass? Mirror? Same deal. Now, my employer is very keen to acquire your 'Looking Glass' and he has instructed me to buy it from you. Apparently it once belonged to a famous writer. That's good news, huh? So think about a figure that to you is a lot of money and maybe we can do business?'

'Well, what if I don't want to sell it?' Alice replied.

'Everything has a price Alice, remember sentiment don't pay the rent.'

Alice thought about her bike. It was three hundred pounds. Could she get three hundred pounds from this strange man? The Looking Glass had only cost thirty but there was no harm in trying.

'How about three hundred?'

There was a long pause on the other end of the line.

'That was stupid! I've messed this up,' thought Alice.

'Are you crazy? Three hundred is far too much. There's no way we could go that high. How about one hundred? Now, you think about that, Miss Liddell. It's a very generous offer.'

Alice was disappointed but one hundred pounds was quite a lot of money and besides, what if the Looking Glass was going to keep giving her these weird dreams? With this in mind one hundred pounds was beginning to sound more attractive.

'One hundred, you said?'

'Yes, to be honest with you, Alice, one hundred thousand is the total top of the budget. Are you ok with that? Do we have a deal?

Alice couldn't believe what she was hearing. One hundred thousand!' but she decided to try and sound casual. Steadying her nerves, she waited before replying yes.

'Okay,...that sounds quite um....okay.'

'Email us the details and we'll transfer the money into any account of your choosing and pick up the mirror - sorry, - Looking Glass tomorrow. It's been nice doing business with you. Have a good night now.'

Still not quite knowing what to make of the conversation, Alice became aware of a slight stinging pain on the underside of her left forearm and so with her free right hand she carefully flicked up the sleeve of her shirt. Clearly visible, from wrist to bicep, was a line of angry red scratches that looked as if they might have been made by the thorns of a rose.

'Maybe sometimes you are meant to find a magical object and maybe sometimes that object is meant to find you', thought Alice as she placed the phone down with a click.

Afterword

The writing of this book has taken a number of years so it might be best to begin at the beginning. Almost a decade ago I was given a notebook by someone very precious to me. She had decorated the cover with fragments of broken mirrored glass and next to this had written, 'Sorry for breaking your HAT Mad Hatter'.

I didn't think too much about it at the time. She had managed to break the brim of a hat I had lying about by pulling it too hard down over her head in a typically determined manner and although I wasn't bothered by the hat's unfortunate new condition, the notebook was given to me by way of an apology.

A couple of years later, when visiting a provincial bookshop, I was offered a Victorian era chessboard and a signed photograph of Sir Winston Churchill. The photograph had probably been requested from Churchill to decorate a local Municipal Office, making it quite a valuable but unremarkable artefact. The chessboard however was interesting. It was made more intringuing by the fact that it had illustrations of characters from Lewis Carroll's Alice stories hand-painted around its border. Although I knew nothing about chessboards, I bought this one because it possessed the sort of faded beauty that often betrays an illustrious past. It was a hot day and I decided to have an al fresco iced coffee, balancing the chessboard against my chair as I drank it. I then got up, paid the bill, and happily drove away, getting about fifteen minutes into my journey before realising I'd left my most intriguing purchase behind.

Luckily when I turned the car around and got back there, the chessboard was still sitting exactly where I'd left it, with other people oblivious to the abandoned stranger in their midst. Later, tired from driving but pleased to be home, I walked up the stairs, through the door, placed the chessboard carefully in a cupboard, and didn't think about it again for about a week.

On a warm summer's morning with light streaming in through the French windows, I decided it would be a good moment to retrieve the chessboard and take a look at it in closer detail. I took it from the cupboard and placed it in the centre of the wooden dining table.

The board was large by modern standards, about two feet square which included a flat border of about three and a half inches width. The border was a distressed silver and had sixteen coloured Alice illustrations around it, each of these framed within a jagged outline resembling broken glass. There were four monogram ink signatures on the board, one in each corner. I wasn't quite sure of the initials, one of the letters was definitely an upper case J with a distinctive hook-shaped cross stroke at the top but the other looked like it might be an italicised Z .

The illustrations themselves seemed more familiar. I couldn't place exactly where but was sure of having seen something very like them somewhere before. Curious for a comparison, I scanned my bookshelves. Luckily I had an edition of *Alice's*

Adventures in Wonderland on a shelf close to hand and opened it on an illustration. Although it was in black and white, the style was strikingly similar to the illustrations on the chessboard. I turned to another page, again the style was identical, but this time the illustration had an illegible signature in the lower part of the plate.

There was a moment of disappointment but then scanning across the page, in the opposite corner, just below the plate, there it was! The exact same monogram as was staring up at me from the chessboard. I turned to the title page which read: *'Alice's Adventures in Wonderland by Lewis Carroll with forty-two illustrations by John Tenniel'*. It wasn't a Z, it was a t for Tenniel, the first and most important illustrator of Alice.

Could this really be John Tenniel's own hand-painted Alice chessboard? That would make it not just an Alice chessboard but The Alice Chessboard. It was exciting. One by one I compared the illustrations on the board to those in the book. Every one of the illustrations in the book looked to have been drawn by the hand that had created the chessboard but none of them depicted the same scenes. In some ways this was a really good sign as even the most sophisticated forgeries are copied from published images, but still it was puzzling. Why would John Tenniel make a chessboard? I could think of no particular reason that he wouldn't, but none why he would either. Then I remembered Lewis Carroll had written another Alice book, a sequel called *Through the Looking-Glass* and I was pretty sure Tenniel had illustrated this as well.

It was the summer of 2011 and I'd been through eighteen months of hell. I do not believe there is a vocabulary to communicate the horror and finality of that experience to someone who has not experienced it themselves, and someone who has will never need to be reminded, but as a result my waking hours were often spent in a sort of somnambulistic daze and the arrival of the chessboard was a welcome distraction.

The door clunked firmly behind me as I went out to find a copy of *Through the Looking-Glass*.

Heading south up the Fulham Road, past the designer flag-ship stores grouped together in their boastful clusters like commercial mean girls, the road relaxes a little. There's the Royal Marsden Hospital, some red brick mansion flats, a vet, and a large but understated and very successful rare book shop. It's the kind of place that you go to if you really want something and are not too bothered about the price. Sure enough, they had a first edition of *Through the Looking-Glass*, in fact they had more than one. I chose the cheapest which was a copy bound in plain red morocco and opened it on the title page:

THROUGH THE LOOKING-GLASS
AND WHAT ALICE FOUND THERE
With fifty illustrations by John Tenniel

This is exactly what I was hoping it would say. The frontis-piece showed Alice talking to a knight on horseback and there was definitely something like this on the chessboard. In a rare moment of self denial, I decided I wouldn't open it again until I got back home. This could have been driven by gambler's su-perstition or simply a desire for privacy but wherever my new found willpower came from, it was just about strong enough to get me through the five minute journey home and up the stairs to my flat. I unwrapped the book, placed it on the table next to the chessboard and began to go through it page by page. One of the very first things that came up was an elegant illustration of a chessboard in traditional chess problem format with: 'White Pawn (Alice) to play and win in eleven moves' printed below.

Now everything began coming back to me. I remembered reading this book as a child; it was darker in tone than *Alice in Wonderland* and chess featured heavily in it. Just a few pages further on was the first direct hit, a picture of the White Knight sliding down a poker. There he was right beside me on the chessboard and he was perfect. In fact, going through the rest of the book, I found all the chessboard illustrations either in roughly the same form, or present in abstracted detail. Then I measured the images to make sure they were a different size to the ones in the book, indicating that no part of them could have been traced.

Normally this would have been the end of it. A Victorian period chessboard with four of the artist's signatures and illustrations that were perfectly executed but markedly different in size and composition to any published versions. It was clearly John Tenniel's, but as the weeks went by I became even more fascinated. I did further research, employing an expert to date the board through forensic pigment analysis, finding differences and similarities that could only be Tenniel's. Then the pigment analysis results came back and they were about as good as they could be. There was no paint like this produced after 1875, and there was no evidence of pencil at all, meaning the illustrations were drawn freehand in ink directly onto the wood. The silver background was in fact white gold leaf laid on very flat so as to look seamless.

At this point it might have been sensible to sell the chessboard but unfortunately I have never been very interested in what is usually considered sensible. This isn't so much a boast as a character defect. Before I knew it I was making an exact replica so as to understand the method of construction.

It took ages finding the best people in their respective fields to work on the project. Even at this stage there seemed to be an acknowledgement of cosmic approval as the crew all sounded famous before we began. Kate Hepburn was the water colourist, Johnnie Walker was hand-cutting the chess squares, Matthew Rich was screen-printing and Ken Brookes was entrusted with the gilding.

Everything was done by hand and everything had to be done properly. I found out that making one chessboard would cost a huge amount of money but if I made them in batches of ten, it went down to just over half the price. So that's what we did; the chessboards when finally finished were brilliant.

Then I needed a shop to sell them from, decorated with objects from my own collection. My girlfriend Jo found Harley, the most beautiful giant white rabbit in the world and travelled to Sheffield to get him.

We sat him in the shop window on a bed of live grass with a leather-studded rabbit hole and the chessboard suspended above him on a perspex shelf. Every morning he would emerge ears first to gasps of disbelief from passers-by.

This book was less ambitious in its infancy. Having opened a shop and created a brand called 'Alice Through The Looking Glass' it seemed natural to me that we publish an edition of the book. My initial idea was to subtly redraw some elements of Tenniel's illustrations and then ask Kate to colour them in a psychedelic palette. The problem was I hadn't read the book since childhood and re-reading it proved a bit of a shock, like discovering the actual lyrics to a song you have misunderstood for years. Some of the chapters had a really saccharine tone to them that I couldn't relate to my memory of the book at all. This meant it could not just be recoloured, I was going to have to rewrite it.

If you start from the proposition that a mirror could be a gateway to inter-dimensional travel, then clearly that mirror would have to possess some sort of magical properties. One of the first things to do was to try and find anything that could link the real Lewis Carroll to magic. I had decided my Alice would be called Alice Liddell after the original inspiration for Carroll's book. This would not only give me another avenue to look for magical connections, but also the opportunity to have her feign to be the disinherited heir to a German supermarket fortune.

I felt that if I could find enough interesting but disparate facts about these two people and arrange them to my own design then, if I was lucky, I might end up with something that read like a potentially believable conspiracy theory.

All my life strange things have happened. What was about to happen next were some of the strangest things yet.

Lewis Carroll died on January 14th 1898, although it could be argued that he had never really lived at all. Lewis Carroll was a pseudonym, the author's real name was Charles Dodgson and he taught mathematics at Christ Church College, Oxford. Like all natural scavengers, the rare book trade thrives on death with even the most distinguished libraries unable to resist the combined pressure of expectant relatives and Her Majesty's Revenue and Customs. Dodgson's estate proved no exception and his personal effects, including furniture, were duly sold off by E.J.Brooks, an Oxford auctioneer on May 10th 1898.

Fortunately, I was able to find a copy of the sale catalogue which on the second day listed numerous works relating to the Occult and supernatural phenomena, including *The Phantom World, Facts in Mesmerism, British Goblins, Wright's Narrative of Sorcery and Magic, The Supernatural in Nature, The Demon, Magic and Magicians,* eleven volumes of *Psychical Research Proceedings* and *The Literature and Curiosities of Dreams.* This proved he had at least a passing interest in magical phenomena but best of all, among the items listed on the first day of the sale, was Lot 63, a gilt-framed mirror or Looking Glass which I could now write into my book.

I decided the next line of enquiry should be Masonic as the Masons hold a particular fascination for the disenfranchised and paranoid and nearly all notable English families have some connection to them. It seemed likely that the Dodgson family would include some Freemasons among its line and, if I was really lucky, maybe even Charles Dodgson himself. Their headquarters is located a short walk from our shop in Covent Garden. Occupying approximately two and half acres of prime London real estate, the building projects a foreboding presence on the immediate skyline. Built in the 1930s in the Art Deco style, there is something almost Stalinist to the scale and muscularity of its exterior.

In contrast to this, the staff at reception were surprisingly welcoming. After signing in I was introduced to the librarian, a small middle-aged lady who showed me up the great marble staircase to the library, and helped me to search through the register of past members. Here the trail went cold, or dead even. There was nothing. In fact, the only thing this exercise had managed to establish was that Charles Lutwidge Dodgson had no obvious connection to Freemasonry whatsoever. Still, at least there was no denying his interest in Magic.

There are two types of Magic. Stage Magic that relies on distraction and sleight of hand to create the illusion of a supernatural event, and Ritual Magic, a quasi-religious system purporting to effect change in the natural world by the repetition of arcane words in a specific order. It was Dodgson's interest in the latter that I wanted to investigate next. Over the years I had heard talk of The Golden Dawn, a magical society with a surprising number of writers represented within its membership.

I didn't know anything about The Golden Dawn but the name suggested both a gilded decadence and the lost opportunity for a better world. After all, if you wake with the birdsong on a summer's morning with the streets ghostly empty and bathed in sunlight, you can still believe that anything could happen. I typed 'Golden Dawn' into the search engine and hit return. 'The Hermetic Order of the Golden Dawn' duly appeared.

The dates were encouraging, founded in 1887 eleven years before Carroll's death meant that Carroll could have easily been aware of it. Reading on, it just got better and better.

The order incorporated elements of Freemasonry but there were major differences, like admitting women as equals in an age where they didn't even have the vote.

Then I saw the name of its founder: *Samuel Liddell MacGregor Mathers* – Master Freemason, Author, Occultist and founder of the Hermetic Order of the Golden Dawn.

At its very centre there was a member of the Liddell family. The real Alice's own family, the same as I'd chosen for my book. Everything was just getting curiouser.

Mathers was born in 1854 at what is now number 108, De Beauvoir Rd, Islington, London N.1. An inauspicious start for someone who would later claim to be King James IV re-incarnate, the Count of Glenstrae and the only true conduit between base humanity and the secret chiefs of the astral plane.

Mathers' history is both fascinating and contradictory. His grandfather, also named Samuel, worked as a weaver and married into the Liddell family when he wed Hannah Liddell at St Giles Church, Great Orton in 1809.

The Liddells were a powerful line with deep ties to the Freemasons. Such was their influence that two Masonic Lodges were named after them. However, the most notable member of the family was not a Freemason, but Alice Pleasance Liddell, Lewis Carroll's muse and 'child friend'. Alice was the dedicatee and reputed model for both Alice books and there is even an acrostic poem at the end of *Through the Looking-Glass* that spells out her name in its entirety. Mathers was only a distant relative of Alice Liddell but the connection is genuine and makes all the other coincidences encountered in the writing of this story that much more remarkable. Samuel Liddell Mathers' use of the name MacGregor was a a later addition and, despite the fact no firm evidence can be found to verify his claim of Highland descent, it is not entirely implausible. The whole MacGregor clan was outlawed in 1603, resulting in a kind of Celtic diaspora with members having to take alternative surnames or face the threat of persecution and even death under the orders of King James VI.

Following the death of his father, the young Mathers moved to Bournemouth with his mother. He was initiated as a Freemason in 1877 at the age of 23 and progressed quickly through the three degrees of Masonry to become a Master Mason a mere eighteen months later. His other interests included fencing, boxing and military tactics, the last of which resulted in him joining the First Hampshire Infantry Volunteers.

Mathers' progress in this field was rather less rapid and although he never rose beyond the rank of private, a photograph exists of him wearing the uniform of a lieutenant. It was during this period that Mathers met Frederick Holland, a metallurgist with a specialism in alchemy and the occult, who introduced him to the study of the Kabbalah. Gradually his interest in Freemasonry began to wane and in 1882 he was admitted into the Societas Rosicruciana in Anglia after meeting Dr Wyn Westcott and Dr William Woodman, both of whom were high-ranking Freemasons visiting Bournemouth in the conduct of their Masonic duties.

Mathers was highly intelligent and, despite not finding his calling in a military career, was able to teach himself several languages. By 1884 he was proficient enough in French to translate *Practical instruction in infantry campaigning exercise* from its original published form. He threw himself into Rosicrucian study with the same degree of application, displaying an extraordinary aptitude for the understanding of ceremonial rituals. Dr Westcott was quick to notice Mathers' potential and encouraged his protégé in the more transcendental aspects of the Rosicrucian tradition.

Mathers as a student proved something of a prodigy and was soon promoted to join the governing body of the S.R.I.A.

After his mother's death in 1885, Mathers moved to Great Percy Street in London's Clerkenwell district. Now, with his rent paid for by Westcott, Mathers was able to fully immerse himself in occult researches. He would walk daily to the British Museum Reading Room which housed the manuscripts he would later use to produce his edition of *The Key of Solomon the King*. As a mark of his character, in this work Mathers chose to excise some material that he felt was potentially dangerous, including a chapter dealing with experiments regarding hate and the destruction of enemies. But for now he had been commissioned by Westcott to translate Knorr Von Rosenroth's *Kabbalah Denudata or Kabbalah Unveiled*. It was during this period that Mathers met Dr Anna Kingsford who would become the dedicatee of his Kabbalah translation.

Anna Kingsford was one of the first English women to obtain a degree in Medicine and the only student of her generation to do so without experimenting on animals. She was an early feminist, vegan and anti-vivisectionist, and it was under her influence that Mathers himself adopted these principles that would remain with him his entire life.

Kingsford was active in the esoteric societies of the period and was known to be a gifted seer. Her visions would come to her in sleep but also in trance-like states of awakening and were later issued in published form as *Clothed by the Sun*. Haunted by the horrific memories of animals being dissected without anaesthetic at the Faculté de Médicine in Paris, Kingsford persuaded Mathers to advise her in preparing magical attacks on various practitioners of vivisection, with the intention to assassinate them. It is not known what effect, if any, this had on the brutish medical research.

In 1887, at around the time of the publication of *'Kabbalah Unveiled'*, discussions were already underway to establish a society for the study of Kabbalistic magic. The Order and its rituals were founded on the discovery of some coded or 'cipher' manuscripts. By tradition, these were either unearthed in an abandoned Masonic store-cupboard and passed on to Dr Woodman, or bought by Woodman directly from a second-hand bookstall on the Farringdon Road in London. Whatever the truth of their origin, it was Westcott who first deciphered them, and Mathers who was given the job of writing up the papers into a workable system of Magic from which to establish the new school, The Hermetic Order of the Golden Dawn.

The Golden Dawn would be governed by the triumvirate of Mathers, Westcott and Woodman but the next step was to recruit new members and these were not difficult to find. The atmosphere of late 19th century London was heavy with the influence of both the decadent movement and the Celtic revival in art and literature. This proved fertile ground for groups offering an alternative to the stifling social and religious orthodoxies of the period. Madame Blavatsky's London Lodge had opened in 1878, whilst the Fabian Society was established in 1884. The Golden Dawn would draw members from both.

1887 was important to Mathers for another reason, it was the year he would meet the beautiful and talented artist, Moina Bergson. Moina was the sister of the philosopher Henri Bergson. She had completed a fine art course at the Slade School and the couple chanced across each other among the Egyptian antiquities of the nearby British Museum which Moina would visit to study.

Moina proved to be a gifted clairvoyant and occult student

and was the first woman to be initiated into the Golden Dawn.

In line with Mathers' enlightened views on the equality of women he had insisted that female members be granted the same rights as men in the new school. Others would soon follow, including leading actress Florence Farr, Constance Wilde (wife of the celebrated playwright), Irish revolutionary Maud Gonne, and Moina's fellow Slade student, Annie Horniman. (Horniman would subsequently use her influence to obtain Mathers the position of assistant librarian at her father's museum in Forest Hill.) Notable amongst the male initiates was the poet and playwright William Butler Yeats, who in his book *Autobiographies* wrote:

'At the British Museum reading-room I often saw a man of thirty-six, or thirty-seven in a brown velveteen coat, with a gaunt resolute face, and an athletic body, who seemed before I had heard his name or knew the nature of his studies, a figure of romance... He was called Liddle Mathers (sic).

He had spoken to me, I think at our first introduction, of a society which sometimes called itself - it had a different name among its members - "The Hermetic Students" and in May or June 1887 I was initiated into that society in a Charlotte Street studio…Mathers was its governing mind, a born teacher and organiser. One of those who incites - less by spoken word than by what they are - imaginative action.'

The Golden Dawn novice would need to pass through various grading tests before graduating to the portal grade and encountering 'The Reception of Light', a process thought to unite them with their Higher Genius, and upon its completion they became recognised as an Adeptus Minor. This was the final stage of training for the Outer Order, but there was an Inner Order, membership of which was yet more difficult to attain. The syllabus of the Outer Order was mainly focused on the study of theoretical Magic whereas members of the Inner Order were engaged in its practical application. Controlling the activities of the Inner Order there was said to be a third Order made up of spectral beings from the Astral Plane.

Mathers and Moina were married in 1890 and lived together for a year in the lodge of the Horniman Museum before Mathers fell out with the management and they moved back to central London. During this time Mathers furthered his understanding of the work of the Elizabethan Magus, John Dee. He developed the rules of the Enochian version of chess with pieces designed by Moina in the form of Ancient Egyptian deities. Though the game was usually structured as a four player variant of standard chess, it was said that Mathers would often play alone across dimensions against invisible Gods.

Dr Woodman died in 1891 and was buried in Willesden Cemetery, where the Royal Horticultural Society erected a memorial to commemorate his talent as a gardener. No one was appointed to replace him and The Golden Dawn was run by Mathers and Westcott from this date on.

It was in the summer of 1892, with Annie Horniman's financial support, that Mathers and Moina moved to Paris to establish a French branch of The Golden Dawn. The couple set up home on the Left Bank, and although they would eventually open a Temple in Paris, Mathers' attention had become focused on an ancient manuscript he had discovered in the Bibliothèque de l'Arsenal. This was the grimoire *The Sacred Magic of Abramelin the Mage*. The translation of this book would become Mathers' most important published work.

Meanwhile the London branch of the Golden Dawn under Westcott was flourishing and Mathers began to feel undermined. By 1896 tensions within the group had come to a head and Annie Horniman withdrew her financial support from the Parisian Temple. Mathers' response was to issue a decree demanding total obedience from the London Adepts and requiring them all to sign an oath of allegiance to him. Mathers claimed he had been contacted one midnight by The Secret Chiefs in the Bois de Bologne who had appointed him Supreme Magus and instructed him to demand this oath of loyalty.

Annie Horniman refused to sign and Mathers expelled her from the Order. In 1897 Westcott was forced to resign from all duties and associations with the Golden Dawn following the discovery of his membership. As a coroner for the Crown it was considered deeply inappropriate for him to be dabbling in the occult. Meanwhile in Paris, Mathers and Moina took to the stage to provide themselves with an income. The Rites of Isis was a series of rituals, interspersed with music and choreography adapted from *The Egyptian Book of the Dead*. They would perform these in Egyptian costume at a small theatre near Saint-Lazare. The performances gained mixed reviews, some of them quite favourable, with Moina in particular being complimented for her beauty and singing voice. Unfortunately a less beautiful presence was looming on the horizon in the form of ex-Cambridge student and aspiring Magician, Aleister Crowley.

A controversial figure even in his youth, Crowley had recently published a collection of erotic poetry which was deemed so obscene that it could only be printed abroad. He was privately wealthy with a distaste for material concerns, his main interests being sex, chess, mountaineering and the occult. Despite the unease expressed by some members, including W.B. Yeats, Crowley was initiated into the Outer Order of the Golden Dawn by Mathers in 1898. By the spring of 1899 Crowley reported that he became. '…aware of the presence of a tremendous spiritual and magical force. It seemed to me to proceed from a man sitting in the east, a man I had not seen before but whom I knew must be Very Honoured Frater Iehi Aour, called among men Allan Bennett…He was esteemed second only to Mathers himself; and was perhaps even more feared…he came straight to me, looked into my eyes and said in penetrating and almost menacing tones: "Little brother, you have been meddling with the Goetia!"(Goetia means howling; but is the technical word employed to all operations of that Magick which deals with gross, malignant or unenlightened forces). I told him rather timidly that "I had not been doing anything of the sort."
"In that case," he replied, "the Goetia has been meddling with you."

Subsequently, Crowley rented a flat at 67-69 Chancery Lane and installed Allan Bennett as his own personal tutor in magic.

157

After this period of intensive study and despite the objections of the London Adepts, he was determined to be initiated into the Inner Order and left for Paris to make representations to Mathers directly. Recognising that he needed a London based ally, Mathers duly acquiesced, initiating Crowley into the Inner Order and despatching him to London to represent his interests. The result was an open rebellion by the London Adepts who expelled Mathers from his own Order and elected a temporary committee to govern in his place. Utilising his tactical expertise, Mathers directed Crowley to mount a lightning raid to lay claim to the Golden Dawn Temple at 36 Blithe Road, Hammersmith, but one committee member in particular was alert to the threat, the poet W.B.Yeats. Yeats made his way to Blithe Rd a day before Crowley, changed the locks and waited with his friend Edward Hunter for the trouble to arrive. Arrive it did in the form of Aleister Crowley dressed in a black hawk's mask, full Highland dress with an enormous gold cross on his breast, and a dagger at his side. He managed to brush past the unimposing figure of Yeats but Edward Hunter was a different proposition. As an experienced amateur boxer he was in good physical condition and Crowley's mystical attack was repelled by more conventional means. What the policeman who attended made of this bizarre scene can only be guessed but the whole episode was eventually resolved in the civil court with Crowley being fined five pounds. It marked the end of the Golden Dawn with different factions going on to form splinter groups including Stella Matutina. Crowley took Mathers' teachings and adapted them into the theories of Magick (Thelema) that he was developing, but as Crowley became increasingly drawn towards the darker areas of the Occult, their relationship broke down completely and a battle for the soul of western esoteric mysticism began. Mathers aimed several psychic attacks at Crowley who countered with his own demon-evoking rituals. These hostilities would sustain long into the new century and would eventually draw Moina into the feud. Mathers' death is as shrouded in mystery as his life. It is as if he simply vanished. Although a death certificate was issued in Paris, dated 21st November 1918, doubts have been raised as to its authenticity as no cause of death is listed, nor is there any record of a body, a grave, or even a headstone.

Rumours persist that he perished in a metaphysical duel with Aleister Crowley, but another theory is that the Mathers persona, like the Comte de Saint Germain before him, was merely a temporary guise of the time-travelling immortal and founder of Rosicrucianism itself, Christian Rosenkreutz.

The Looking-Glass trial.

'Aleister Crowley, The Great Beast,' was dubbed the wickedest man in the world, by the press of his day - a reputation that would endure well into the second half of the twentieth century. As well as being a powerful magician he was also an accomplished chess player even managing a draw against British champion Joseph Henry Blackburne. The archetype and epitome of to-day's Rock and Roll clichés, Crowley enjoyed and played up to his reputation for satanic malevolence. Such was the opprobrium attached to Crowley's name that the chemist and former Golden Dawn member George Jones sued the Looking-Glass magazine for libel for merely suggesting that Jones was his associate. Mathers appeared as a witness for the defence and at points in his testimony the proceedings descended into farce causing Judge Justice Scrutton to remark that the trial was 'getting very much like the trial in Alice in Wonderland'.

Crowley refused to testify for Jones and Jones unsurprisingly lost the case. Despite his continued notoriety Crowley died broken and drug addicted with only the pet rabbits of Netherwood (a Hastings boarding house) for company whilst Mathers' fate remains a mystery.

Extracted from 'Towards the Golden Dawn' The Confessions of Aleister Crowley' published 1929.

'During this time, magical phenomena were of constant occurrence. I had two temples in my flat; one white, the walls being lined with six huge mirrors, each six feet by eight; the other black, a mere cupboard, in which stood an altar supported by the figure of a Negro standing on his hands. The presiding genius of this place was a human skeleton, which I fed from time to time with blood, small birds and the like. The idea was to give it life, but I never got further than causing the bones to be covered with a viscous slime. The demons connected with Abra-Melin do not wait to be evoked; they come unsought.

One night Jones and I went out to dinner. I noticed on leaving the white temple that the latch of its Yale lock had not caught.

Accordingly, I pulled the door to and tested it. As we went out, we noticed semi-solid shadows on the stairs; the whole atmosphere was vibrating with the forces we had been using (we were trying to condense them into sensible images.) When we came back, nothing had been disturbed in the flat; but the temple door was wide open, the furniture disarranged and some of the symbols flung about in the room. We restored order and then observed that semi-materialized beings were marching around the main room in almost un-ending procession. When I finally left the flat for Scotland, it was found that the mirrors were too big to take out except by the way of the black temple. This had, of course, been completely dismantled before the workmen arrived. But the atmosphere remained and two of them were put out of action for several hours. It was almost a weekly experience, by the way, to hear of casual callers fainting or being seized with dizziness, cramp or apoplexy on the staircase. It was a long time before those rooms were re-let.

Sir John Tenniel illustrates 'Through the Looking Glass and what Alice found there'.

Lewis Carroll first approached Sir John Tenniel to illustrate *Through the Looking-Glass* in 1866, only a year after the first publication of *Alice in Wonderland*. The working relationship between Carroll and Tenniel had been fraught with tension due to Carroll's fastidious nature and Tenniel's reluctance to be dictated to in his own field of expertise. Despite the enormous success of the first Alice book, Tenniel did not relish the prospect of having to work with Carroll again and offered many excuses and even a flat refusal before finally relenting in June 1868. However, his initial reluctance reflected itself in the progress of the book and when Carroll called on him in March 1869 he was dismayed to find that work had still not begun.

In fact it would take a further two years to complete the illustrations and tellingly upon finishing them Tenniel would almost entirely give up on the illustration of books.

With his brilliant depictions it can be argued that Tenniel is as much the father of the Alice totem as Carroll himself and his influence on *Through the Looking-Glass* was such that not only did Carroll change the action in the railway carriage scene at his suggestion but also excised an entire episode titled *'The Wasp in a Wig'*. Sir John Tenniel's own father, John Baptist Tenniel was of Huguenot descent. The Huguenots were French Protestants fleeing religious persecution under Catholic rule and were from a demographic of skilled craftsmen and professionals. John Baptist had studied under the Italian master of arms, Domenico Angelo and subsequently made a living instructing young men in the skills deemed necessary for a gentleman of the time. Athletic classes like fencing, boxing and rowing were represented in the curriculum but also gentler pursuits like learning the latest waltz.

The young John was brought up in this atmosphere of refined masculinity and it would shape his character as a man. He became a proficient swordsman, athlete and equestrian but his real passion lay elsewhere. Without encouragement from his father, Tenniel taught himself to draw, developing his technique in hours of solitary study and concentration. In other respects he was less introvert with a love of theatre that would culminate in well-received performances for Charles Dickens' amateur theatre company. The Tenniel's were friendly with the artist John Martin and his family, John Tenniel and Leopold Martin became great friends. Together they would spend days sketching from illustrated books in the British Museum.

Tenniel was particularly interested in antique armour and found that once sketched he had an extraordinary ability to memorise details and recall them. Both of the Alice books benefit from the time spent developing this skill but it is most noticeably evident in the illustrations for *Through the Looking-Glass.*

Lillie Rd. Hammersmith, June 2017

Most people would imagine that book dealers exhibit at book fairs to sell books.

To an extent this is true, but the real attraction is the opportunity to buy at the set-up before the public are allowed in. I wasn't exhibiting at the Ibis Hotel, Hammersmith in June and so didn't have much expectation for what I might find as I walked in.

There were upwards of 30,000 books on display but dealers from all over the world had already had seven hours to comb the shelves before my arrival. Although it was considered a relatively minor event they were running a shuttle bus service from the main fair at Olympia which was adding to the competition and to make matters worse, I was running late. Moving quickly around the room I had picked up a few books that seemed reasonably priced but nothing exciting when I came up to a display of books that included an anonymous-looking Victorian Scrap Album. These types of keepsakes were kept by nearly every middle class family of the period and as a result are very common. I don't know why I felt drawn to this volume, maybe it was because it was in a glass case but it had no enticing description and was not opened on any of its pages.

'What's that album in the case?' I heard myself asking without further thought.

'Oh that, that's a Tenniel thing'.

'Tenniel?' I said, 'Sounds interesting, can I have a look?'

He handed me the book. Picking it up I could see the spine

read 'COSTUME' in simple gilt lettering. Opening the covers revealed that Tenniel's Times obituary had been placed loosely inside and a note on a card that read:

'This is one of the late Sir John Tenniel's costume sketchbooks. It belongs to Miss Cicely King. W.H. Rylands Sept. 1917.'

I started leafing through the book. There were pages and pages of highly finished pencil sketches of costume and armour. This wasn't just a Tenniel thing, it was Tenniel's British Museum sketchbook. Although it pre-dated his work on Alice, there was a really impressive depiction of a knight on horseback which I was sure I could use for my rewrite of *Through the Looking-Glass*. This would give me at least one totally new illustration by the artist who created Alice. I was going to have to try and buy it.

'Has anyone else seen this ?' I asked the dealer curiously.

'No, nobody else has really looked at it. It's been in the same family for a hundred years, I only bought it at the weekend'.

There was the price to consider: £12,500. I counted approximately 250 sketches, some finished in watercolour so even using a crude valuation that was only fifty pounds a drawing. It was worth more than that. But the problem was £10,000 was about all the money I had in the world, meaning I was going to have to negotiate. The standard trade discount is 10% but I was going to need a bigger discount or else money would be difficult for a while.

An honest appeal to sympathy might be a good start.

'Okay', I said. 'What is the absolute death on this for a cheque right now? It's really nice but I'm not feeling very rich at the moment.'

He thought for a minute before saying, 'I can't do nine'.

Despite being a negative statement it was actually quite promising, he couldn't do nine, but nine thousand one hundred and fifty wasn't nine, maybe that was a number he could do. Before I'd finished thinking of how to suggest this randomly precise figure he came back with his own price.

'Nine fifty.'

'Er…What?……. Nine fifty…' Nine hundred and fifty pounds! Was I hearing right?

I looked at the price again it was £1250. I had added a nought in my reading of the figure. This was understandable. Firstly the room was dimly lit and I wasn't wearing glasses and secondly why would it be £1250? This would value the drawings at £5 each.

The most important thing to do in a situation like this is act normal. That is, behave as if there's still a decision to be considered. I waited for what seemed like an appropriate amount of time whilst trying to look like I was thinking about something other than 'this is absolutely brilliant' before saying 'Yeah, that seems very fair,' and writing out the cheque.

Two illustrations from the sketchbook which have been newly coloured by Kate Hepburn appear in this book.

22nd December 2015

Aleister Crowley purchased Boleskine House on Loch Ness as a mystical power base to develop and practise rituals from *The Book of Sacred Magic of Abra-Melin the Mage* leading up to what he dubbed the Great Operation (an attempt to establish mystical communion with the Godhead). The house was later bought by Led Zeppelin guitarist and Crowley enthusiast, Jimmy Page. Page sold Boleskine but still owns one of the most important collections of Crowley manuscript material in the world. One of my aims when attempting this rewrite was to make the magical parts as accurate as possible, to the degree that even the spells are based on real ones, so when it came to describing Boleskine I was going to need some images of the house and an understanding of its layout.

I tapped Boleskine House into my laptop and hit search. There were quite a lot of helpful results but strangely, as I started to write the Crowley invocation scene, the search engine began updating with the breaking news that Boleskine House was on fire. I clicked into the report. There was no mention of Aleister Crowley or the house's unusual past, just that a major fire was taking place and was now raging out of control. The house was burnt to the ground and has not been rebuilt since.

I later discovered that both Alice books were required reading for neophyte students of Crowley's magickal system. Self published at Boleskine was Crowley's *'Sword of Song'* which begins with a parody of *Through the Looking-Glass* containing dialogue between Alice and the White Knight:

'You are sad!' the Knight said in an anxious tone; 'let me sing you a song to comfort you.'

'Is it very long?' Alice asked.

'It's long,' said the Knight 'but it's very, very beautiful. The name of the song is called *'The Book of the Beast.'*

Top deck of the no.19 bus Piccadilly, London.

'You'll never guess what?' Jo announced. 'My boss's family own Alice Liddell's mirror.'

'Really?' I replied, 'that's quite a coincidence. Do you think we could borrow it?'

She said she'd investigate the possibility.

The truth was slightly more complicated, Jo's boss's family helped to run a charity that in turn ran a museum which owned the mirror. But it was a good lead.

The New Forest Centre in Lyndhurst is a small scale museum and educational resource dedicated to the history of the New Forest and surrounding area.

Alice Liddell married Reggie Hargreaves, a wealthy cricketer, in 1880 and lived most of her adult life at Cuffnells, a grand country house on the outskirts of Lyndhurst. After Reggie died the family's fortunes gradually declined to the point that by the 1920s Alice was forced to sell the manuscript of *Alice's Adventures Underground* to assist with Cuffnells upkeep. Even the large sum this fetched at auction was not enough to stave off the inevitable and the house was eventually demolished and the contents sold. A local dentist bought Alice's overmantel mirror with the intention of extracting the mercury from the back of its glass for use in dental fillings.

It seems he later abandoned this unromantic project and donated the mirror to the New Forest Centre which is where we found it, propped up in a corner without too much ceremony. The Museum Board were very helpful and for a donation to the museum we managed to secure the mirror on loan to display in our shop. Before leaving Lyndhurst we decided to visit

Alice Liddell's grave. She's buried in the churchyard close to the museum and as we stood at her graveside on this overcast afternoon, bright beams of sunlight burst through the clouds above and bathed us in an ethereal light. The omens seemed good.

THE GRAVE OF
MRS REGINALD HARGREAVES
THE "ALICE" IN LEWIS CARROLL'S
"ALICE IN WONDERLAND"

Alice Through The Looking Glass,14 Cecil Court, London

I was sitting at the desk staring at the computer and thinking about all the coincidences that had occurred during the writing of this book.

Not only had I found Sir John Tenniel's *Through the Looking-Glass* chessboard and now his lost sketchbook but I had also been drawn into a legal dispute with the Walt Disney Corporation that was nearing its conclusion. The case centred on the marketing of goods relating to a film called 'Alice Through The Looking Glass' produced by Tim Burton and starring Johnny Depp.

With neither side backing down we seemed destined for our own Looking-Glass trial and it was scheduled to be heard only yards from the flat in Chancery Lane where Crowley had once attempted to re-animate a human skeleton. Weirdly, some years earlier my son had been cast in a film directed by Tim Burton in which he played Johnny Depp as a child.

Given the nature of some of my other discoveries it was all beginning to feel a little unsettling. I knew that Carl Jung attributed a lot of meaning to coincidence in his psychoanalytic theory. Maybe my Alice should be having a recurrent bad dream and this would explain why she was tired and had done so badly in her exam? The trouble was that I didn't really know any detail of Jung's ideas concerning dreams. What I did know was that his collected works ran to something like twenty volumes and the idea of working my way through these was not an appealing prospect.

I needed someone who could offer a simple explanation of the types of dream imagery that Jung would have considered significant. At this moment my thoughts were interrupted by a female voice.

'Can I try on the rabbit mask?'

It was summer and I hadn't noticed her breeze in through the open door.

'Yes, you can if you're careful not to leave make-up on the inside,' I replied.

We had commissioned these masks as a sort of haute couture party accessory and despite our insistence on faux fur, they were still expensive to produce.

'Don't worry, I will probably buy it anyway.'

I took the mask down from on top of the display cabinet and handed it to her.

She tied it behind her head and walked over to look at herself in Alice Liddell's mirror, tilting her head at various angles to gauge the effect.

'Did you know the rabbit is a symbol of coincidence?' she asked in her rabbit guise.

'No, no I didn't. Is that the reason there's a rabbit in Donnie Darko?'

She ignored this question and answered one that I hadn't yet asked.

'I am going to put it in my office for client consultations.'

'Really, that's unusual, I think most people buy them for parties. Are you a doctor?'

'Not exactly, I'm a therapist.'

'That could be very helpful. Do you know anything about Carl Jung?'

'I would hope so,' she replied ' I'm a Jungian psychotherapist.'

Even when seeking to understand coincidence, I was presented with another coincidence. She explained her own story, how she had travelled to California from her home in rural France to seek a blonde woman who kept appearing in her dreams. She said that somehow she intuitively knew that this was the path that she must follow.

She met the blonde woman by complete chance while hitch-hiking. The woman would later become famous as the singer in Fleetwood Mac. She also met her husband, a record producer, and with her life shaped by the decision to abandon everything and follow a dream, it seemed natural to undergo her own psychoanalytic journey. From there she started her practice. She asked if there was somewhere good for coffee and so I suggested an artisan cafe next to the Opera House in Saint Martin's Lane. We sat down at one of the wooden benches and found her husband was sitting at the next table. She introduced me.

'Have you two arranged to meet?' I said, rather confused that she would ask for a recommendation, having already arranged to meet him there, but it turned out to be completely random and neither of them had been to the café before nor were they planning to go there that day. He was interviewing a singer who had chosen the café because of its musical theme. He excused himself and went back to his table.

We finished our coffees and returned to the shop.

Before she left I decided to gift her the mask on the condition that she explain the meaning of my coincidences.

She started with an obscure quote from Rilke regarding the influence of the stars but then moved on to synchronicity and how the Native Americans see the rabbit as a messenger with the ability to travel between dimensions, bringing with it the gift of prophecy and creative intuition. Her parting words were:

'It's very simple, your book is not about magic, it is magic and you must finish it.'

Additional notes to the text

'Carved at its base were the initials DEDI'
DEDI

Daemon Est Deus Inversus, DEDI in abbreviation, was the magical name adopted by the poet W.B.Yeats during his membership of the Hermetic Order of the Golden Dawn.

This ancient Kabbalistic motto translates as 'The Devil is God Inverted', referring to the opposing forces required for balance and harmony in the world, as with Light and Dark, or Life and Death. Good cannot exist without its mutually dependent opposite, Evil and an image will always reflect in reverse.

'Purchased for Stella Matutina from the Dodgson sale of 1898'
Stella Matutina (Morning Star)

An early twentieth century magical order founded by Robert Felkin and dedicated to the teachings of the Hermetic Order of the Golden Dawn.

With strong representation from the Edwardian literary world, Stella Matutina could count E.Nesbit, author of *The Railway Children* as one of its early members as well as W.B.Yeats.

'Thought once to have been the property of Bishop Berkeley'
Bishop Berkeley

George Berkeley was an Irish-born Anglican bishop and one of the most influential philosophers of the eighteenth century.

Bishop Berkely is best known for his theory of Immaterialism, arguing that matter does not exist and that even familiar objects are merely a collection of ideas existing only in the mind of the person who perceives them, a notion encapsulated in the phrase 'esse est percipi' (to be is to be perceived).

'Bishop captures Rook. Hmm, I wonder why he's done that?'
The Immortal Game

This game was played between Adolf Anderssen (White) and Lionel Kieseritzky (Black) at Simpsons-in-the-Strand, London on 21 June 1851 and remains one of the most famous encounters in the history of chess. Characterised by Anderssen's ingenious sacrificing of major pieces in order to develop play and secure eventual victory, it soon after became known as 'The Immortal Game'. The 18th move Bishop captures rook on g1 is from the later stages of the game and is considered to be decisive in ensuring Kieseritzky's defeat. Although Kieseritzky has an extra two rooks and a Bishop which would normally convey an overwhelming material advantage, Anderssen's active pieces counteract this. Kieseritzky was check-mated five moves later.

'An embroidered rampant lion stared out defiantly above its entrance with the words Deo duce comite ferro below.'
Deo Duce Comite Ferro (God as my guide, my companion a sword)

One of the magical pseudonyms of Samuel Liddell Macgregor Mathers. Another was the Scottish Gaelic 'S Rioghail Mo Dhream' which translates as 'Royal is my race', the slogan of the chiefs of the Macgregor clan.

'Alice placed her right foot directly over its head. Now that she had all the power, Alice could extinguish this creature's life with one stamp and for a split second she considered it.

Eliphas Levi

Eliphas Levi was a French 19th century occultist whose works on ritual magic were a major influence on Samuel Liddell Macgregor Mathers and the teachings of the Golden Dawn. In his book 'Transcendental Magic' he states 'Two things as we have already said, are necessary for the acquisition of magical power - the emancipation of the will from all servitude, and its instruction in the art of domination. The sovereign will is represented in our symbols by the woman who crushes the serpent's head, and by the radiant angel who restrains and constrains the dragon with lance and heel. In this place let us affirm without evasions that the great magical agent - the dual current of light, the living and astral fire of the earth was represented by the serpent with the head of an ox, goat, or dog, in ancient theogonies. It is the double serpent of the caduceus, the old serpent of Genesis, but is also the brazen serpent of Moses, twisted round the tau , that is the generating lingam.

It is further, the goat of the Sabbath and the Baphomet of the Templars; it is the Hyle of the Gnostics; it is the double tail of the serpent which forms the solar cock of Abraxas. In fine, it is the devil of M. Eudes de Mirville, and is really the blind force which souls must overcome if they would be free from the chains of earth; for unless their will can detach from this fatal attraction, they will be absorbed in the current by the force which produced them, and they will return to the central and eternal fire. The whole magical work consists, therefore, in our liberation from the folds of the ancient serpent, then in setting a foot upon its head and leading it where we will.'

Some time after completing the writing of this book I was curious to look up how Carl Jung himself explained synchronicity. The result was extraordinary, of all the examples he could have used to illustrate his concept he chose to quote from a book, and the book he chose was Lewis Carroll's *Through The Looking-Glass:*

'It's a poor sort of memory that only works backward. The rule is, jam tomorrow and jam yesterday- but never jam today.'

'It must sometimes come to jam today,' Alice objected.

'No it can't,' said the Queen. 'It's jam every other day; today isn't any other day, you know.'

'I don't really understand what you mean. It's quite confusing.'

'That's the effect of living backwards', the Queen said kindly. 'It always makes one a little giddy at first.'

'Living backwards!' Alice repeated in astonishment.

'But the one great advantage to it. is one's memory works both ways.'

'I'm sure mine only works one way,' said Alice, 'when it works at all.'

'It's a very poor sort of memory that only works backwards,' the Queen remarked.

'What sort of things do you remember best?' Alice ventured.

'Oh, things that happened the week after next,' the Queen replied nonchalantly.

Acknowledgements

Thanks to Kate Hepburn for the beautiful colouring of nearly all of these images. To E.A.P. who drew the extraordinary demons that appear in this book, on 6th August 1847, Clerkenwell, London.

With additional thanks to Jo Humphris, Jane Fior, Harley, Robin Jwaher Whitehead, David Banks, James Riley, Roman Silberfeld, Benjamin Kingston, Geoffrey Hobbs, Ben Weinreich, Susan Snell and The Freemasons' Grand Lodge, Covent Garden.

Turning and turning in the widening gyre
The falcon cannot hear the falconer;
Things fall apart; the centre cannot hold
Mere anarchy is loosed upon the world...'

W.B. Yeats, The Second Coming